THE AMISH COWBOY'S BABY

Montana Millers · Book 2

ADINA SENFT

Moonshell
Books

Cover design by Carpe Librum Book Design. Images used under license.

Quotations from the King James Version of the Holy Bible.

The Amish Cowboy's Baby / Adina Senft—1st ed.

ISBN 978-1-950854-20-2

❀ Created with Vellum

INTRODUCTION

THE AMISH COWBOY'S BABY

A lonely prodigal, a cowboy rebel, a secret baby.
A recipe for disaster ... or for unexpected love?

Joshua Miller is the youngest in the Miller family—and the one most likely to break his mother's heart. The minute he can sneak away, he's out with his *Englisch* friends, planning when he'll jump the fence. It's all good times and bad choices ... until the day he finds a baby at the door with a note saying the child is his.

Sara Fischer once thought the grass was greener on the other side, only to discover that coming back to the church can be harder than leaving it. Now she's returned to Montana ranch country, where the only job she can find is on the Circle M—as a nanny. She may not be very good with babies, but she knows a hurting man when she sees one—and she responds to Joshua in a way she never has with anyone else.

The Amish way of life is the fence that divides them. But can a baby's trusting smile be the key that opens their hearts to each other—and to God?

The Montana Millers. They believe in faith, family, and the land. They'll need all three when love comes to the Circle M!

THE AMISH COWBOY'S BABY

1

MOUNTAIN HOME, MONTANA

For unto us a child is born, unto us a son is given.
—Isaiah 9:6

DAT WAS RIGHT. For everything you did outside the will of God, there was a price to pay.

Joshua Miller, in the fifth year of his *Rumspringe*, was so hungover he thought his pounding head might come off and roll across the floor. He groaned as he attempted to lift it high enough to squint out the window. The sun was up. And he was alone. But where? When?

Rumspringe was supposed to be fun. Not to hurt this bad.

He looked down at himself. Still dressed. Huh.

The bed covers weren't familiar. Neither was the room.

Maybe, instead of rolling over and going back to sleep the way he wanted to, he ought to find out where he was. He remembered the party in Whitefish with the Madison brothers and a bunch of their ski friends. Then coming home yesterday and freezing his toes off going ... somewhere ... in the back of the big Ford pickup with some kids from town.

The rail trestle, maybe? Had they taken the truck out on the frozen lake?

Nope. He had nothing. Just a big blank expanse where a good time should have been.

Josh rolled to his feet. He found the door and opened it, and recognition flooded in. By some miracle he'd wound up in the ranch hands' bunkhouse at the Rocking Diamond, the dude ranch and stud farm owned by Brock and Taylor Madison. Most of the hands had either been laid off for the winter months or gone home for Christmas, which was why he'd probably crawled up the steps and into the nearest bed he could find. And how about that—his phone was still in his back pocket.

Sunday, December 13, 10:42 a.m.

Oh, boy. If he didn't hoof it back to the Circle M, he'd not only be assigned some awful job as punishment for missing church, he'd get something even worse for not being home when the family drove in after the fellowship meal. But if he could get his head together long enough to find some helpful chore to do, maybe that would lower *Dat*'s anger levels into the orange zone instead of the red.

He couldn't risk being kicked off the ranch. He needed every penny he could save to go to Seattle and start a new life. An *Englisch* life. He had his share of the money from the cows they'd sold last autumn, and Tyler Carson had said that after Christmas, he'd buy Joshua's share of the car they co-owned. With that, he'd be on a bus the first chance he got, leaving this place behind.

He found his coat on the floor on top of his boots, his wallet still in the pocket. He filled a quart canning jar he found in the kitchen with water from the tap, and drank it down. Every step on the exterior staircase of the bunkhouse was torture, and it only got worse as he hiked the five miles cross-country to the Circle M. The morning was almost mild—a warm wind had come up from the west, creating a Chinook arch made of clouds over the mountains, with the wind blowing through it.

Already the snow left on the ground from the last storm had begun to melt. If this kept up, they'd have clear roads for once. By the last mile his head was clearing, too, as he breathed in the scent of pines and wet earth. He cut through *Grossmammi*'s orchard and zigzagged down the path to the Miller house on its knoll, then took the steps two at a time up to the deck. From here he had a staggering view of the valley below, mostly covered in snow yet, but he could see the frozen river where the snow had blown off. Mountains stood guard, blue and purple peaks white with snow, their sides fringed with green pines.

But he couldn't stand around admiring the view. He had to get cleaned up and changed and find something to do before his parents' buggy came rolling up the lane.

He opened the door of the narrow boot room that gave on to the house proper, and blinked.

There was something sitting just inside, on the waterproof mat. A present of some kind?

His parents were friendly with all the *Englisch* in the valley, but they didn't have the sort of relationships that led to presents left on the porch at Christmas. An Amish family would never just drop a gift and run—certainly not on a Sunday. No, they'd come in the evening, be invited in and given something to eat, and two hours would go by while everyone caught up with the news of people they'd probably just seen in church that week.

He closed the door and stood there with his hands on his

hips, staring down at a wicker basket with a bunch of blankets rolled up in it.

And then something punched the blanket from inside and yelled, and Joshua nearly fell over backward as he stumbled away from it. "What in the blazes?"

It looked like kittens were playing under there. Sounded like it, too.

"*Ach, neh,*" he said in tones of disgust. "Tell me somebody hasn't dumped a litter on us." He was half tempted to take the basket down to the river and toss it in. How many were in there? And how old?

He pulled away the soft blue blanket that had been carefully tucked into the sides of the basket.

A small human face, screwed up in frustration, met his disbelieving gaze. A pair of blue eyes focused on him. And then a wail, not as loud as the first one, as if it had been going at it for a while and had given up hope that anyone was listening.

Joshua took the Lord's name in vain. Several times. Loudly.

"Who thought it was a good idea to leave a baby in the boot room in December?" he demanded of the basket.

He snatched it up and got it into the warmth of the house. It was only about fifty-five degrees out, but still, babies were supposed to be warm. What on earth was going on?

He swore again as he set his burden on the kitchen table. He'd seen enough babies to know that this one was probably three or four months old. "We have to get you back where you belong, because it sure ain't here. Where is *Mamm* when I need her?"

At the Burkholders', that was where, way on the other side of the valley.

There were lumps under the blankets. One by one he pulled them out.

Bottles. Full of milk.

Oh, no. This did not look good. This meant somebody was counting on the baby being here at least a day. Maybe more.

His questing fingers around the baby's warm, squirming body in its tiny blue snow suit located something else. Not more bottles. An envelope.

He pulled it out. His name was written on the front.

No, no, no.

Sunday, December 13

Dear Joshua,

You probably don't remember me, but it doesn't matter. We had a night together back around New Year's, and this is the result. Meet Nathan Joshua Miller. I know he's yours because I hadn't been with anyone for months before that, and believe me, I don't plan on it for years after this.

I got accepted to university and won't be coming back. There's no room in my life for a child. My parents don't even know I had him. They thought I was doing a couple of exchange terms in Boston.

I know the Amish are all about family so the best place for him is with his dad. His birth certificate is enclosed. I hope you love him like he deserves. Even as messed up as you are, you have to be a better dad than I would be a mom.

Carey Lindholm

Joshua's mouth hung open, the shock like ice water cascading over his head, his shoulders, all the way to his feet. Then going to his insides, like ice breaking and causing a flood.

He dropped the letter on the table and lunged for the

kitchen sink, where he was violently sick, enough to rid himself of every bad decision from last night. The sudden movement must have scared the baby, because it let out a shriek.

Then it started to cry.

That made two of them.

2

THE BUS ROARED up in front of the tiny station in Mountain Home, Montana, and jerked to a halt in one of the two long parking spaces. Sara Fischer woke up with a jolt as her head smacked against the window.

"Ow." She rubbed the sore spot, groggy from lack of sleep, and blinked some moisture into her eyes. Not that it did much good. It still felt like someone had thrown sand into them.

Mountain Home didn't seem to have changed much in the years since she'd left. The bus station still needed its windows washed. The Gas-N-Go was still painted banana yellow for reasons no one understood. And there was Talley's bar, the only one in town, looking exactly the way it had the last time she'd stumbled out of it. The sign in the window said OPEN in loopy neon letters. Of course it was.

They said you couldn't go home again. Well, sometimes you could. Sometimes you didn't have a choice.

With a sigh, she collected her backpack from the overhead rack and made sure her zipped wallet was still in the inside pocket of her puffy jacket. Fact was, she was coming home pretty much the way she'd left, except then she hadn't had a backpack. All her worldly goods had been stuffed in two canvas grocery bags with rope handles. *Mamm* had made them.

Nope. Not going to think about that.

She went into the bus station's only bathroom and pulled out the clothes she'd put on top inside the pack. That she'd hung on to for reasons even she couldn't explain. Then she stripped out of her jeans and sweatshirt and put them on. Black tights. A purple dress that still fastened up the front with snaps, though they pulled a little across the chest now. It was too short now, too, but that couldn't be helped. An apron, though she had to use safety pins because the original straight pins were long gone. She had no idea where she'd lost the cape. Her white, bucket-shaped *Kapp* had been torn off her head in a wind storm somewhere in Olympia. So all she had was a *Duchly*, a scarf, bought at the dollar store.

Sara tied it over her hair. That would be the second thing someone noticed. The hair, cropped short.

She gazed at herself in the mirror. *You look like you put on an Amish Halloween costume with half the pieces missing.*

Yep, pretty much.

She pulled her cowboy boots back on because where did you buy black Oxfords outside of an Amish store? Besides, they were good boots. She didn't plan on giving them up. But she had left Amish, so she'd come back that way.

Back to the only life that seemed even remotely familiar. Back to make up for her mistakes. To try again.

She walked through the tiny downtown, feeling out of place and far too visible. In *Englisch* clothes no one would have noticed her. In Amish clothes, the same. But in this half-and-half outfit, she stood out.

She also stood out because she was the only one on the street, despite the unseasonable warmth in the air. And then she realized why—it was Sunday. Half the shops in Mountain Home seemed to be Amish now, which meant they were closed. But on a closer look, the town had changed. It looked downright prosperous. The Rose Garden Quilt Shop. Yoder's Variety Store. The Dutch Apple Café. Mountain Carpentry and Cabinets.

The Amish seemed to have turned the town around. That was a good sign. That meant there might be work.

Her heart kicked as she passed a window full of candles. She stopped. Leaned in to get a better look at the display. Pillar candles with flowers and leaves embedded in creamy wax were surrounded by wreaths of holly and fat bows made of red and gold ribbon. Behind them and tucked in between were books—at least a dozen Christmas romances with happy couples on the covers. She glanced up at the old-fashioned swinging sign, hanging over the boardwalks just like the ones over the other shops.

CURRER BELL'S BOOKS AND CANDLES.

Okay, not Amish, clearly. But the shop was in the same location as the previous one where her mother had sold her candles. Maybe these folks had bought it after—

She jerked into motion and walked on, down to the end of the street where it turned back into a highway and continued on out into ranch country. End of the line. Fine. She turned and walked back to the only place that seemed to be open.

Talley's.

She paused inside the door. It took a few seconds for her eyes to adjust from the brilliant day outside to the dim lighting that did more to hide spills and scuffs than it did to illuminate anything. Not one thing had changed. She tripped over the board that stuck up next to the tiny raised stage and shook her head at herself. At one time she'd stepped over it instinctively.

"Help you?" The man behind the bar took her in. "Hey, Sara. That you?"

"Hi, Leroy."

"You back in town for good?"

"I'm not sure I can manage good. But I'm back."

"Staying at your folks' place, I guess. Hope you have a fall-back plan. No one's been out there in years. Except kids, maybe."

Her stomach sank, as did her shoulders. She hadn't really thought about what happened to empty houses. "Guess I'll find out."

"You got a car?"

She shook her head. "I just got off the bus. I'll walk." It was a long way. But again—no choice.

He leaned over the counter. "Hey, Miller."

A boy lifted his head like it weighed fifty pounds. Amish kid, Sara saw at once. On *Rumspringe*, obviously. He looked completely miserable, despite the fact that two others at the table were hollering at the TV, cheering on some football team. There was a basket at his feet.

"You and Tyler Carson still own that car together?" Leroy asked him.

He nodded.

"Why don't you take Sara here out to the old Fischer place? You're probably the only one in here besides me who isn't over the limit."

He hesitated, as though he didn't want to give up his roaring good time to do somebody a favor.

"It's okay—" she began, when the kid pulled his black wool

coat off the back of his chair, shrugged into it, and picked up the basket.

"Come on. Tyler's place is only a couple blocks from here." He trudged out the door without waiting for Sara to agree or disagree or drop dead.

Leroy shrugged. "Up to you."

Her other option was to belly up to the bar in her Amish dress and order a beer. But that wasn't happening ever again, no matter how much the day called for it. She nodded her thanks, reseated her backpack on one shoulder, and followed the Miller kid out.

She caught up to him at the end of the block. "What's in the basket?"

"A baby."

She must have misheard. "A baby what?"

"A baby ... baby." He lengthened his stride, but she was as tall as he was and didn't have any trouble matching it. She *was* having trouble with the basket.

"Why are you carting a baby around town in a basket?"

"Because I don't know what else to do with it and my mother's not home from church yet."

This made no sense whatsoever. "So your first thought was to go to Talley's?"

"I got a ride. This was where they were going."

She eyed him. "Your logic skills need work. Whose baby is it?"

"Mine, apparently. I found it on our front porch about an hour and a half ago. Him. His name is Nathan."

"Which you know because ..."

"His birth certificate is in the basket."

Of course it was. The mother was capable of logic, anyway. "Did you feed him?"

"Yeah. She put some bottles in with him. He drank one."

"She who? His mom?"

"I guess. Here's Tyler's place. If you take the baby I'll drive."

"Not a chance. I don't know how much you've had to drink. Besides, I know where we're going. I also know that if you've really got a baby in there, you're supposed to have a car seat."

"He'll have to go on the floor, then, because I don't."

The car was an old Swinger and the key lay on top of the left front tire, just where he told her. There wasn't much Sara could do but make sure the basket was secure between the kid's feet and hope to goodness the state patrol didn't stop them for a broken taillight or something.

It felt strange to drive the familiar meandering roads across the valley in a car, not a buggy. Particularly a car with an engine this powerful under its rusty hood. It took ten minutes instead of an hour, which was a shame, because she wasn't exactly looking forward to arriving.

The car bumped up the lane. At least there were no recent tire tracks in the dirty snow.

"You know people here?" The kid was staring out the window. "Isn't this the old Fischer place?"

"Yes. I'm Sara Fischer."

He gawked at her as though he recognized the name. "You're the one who—"

"Yes. I never did get your name."

It took him a second to recover from recollecting who she was. "Joshua. Josh Miller. My parents are Reuben and Naomi, on the Circle M ranch."

She'd been to church there many a time. Sat in that big

living room looking out on God's creation and never doubted that she'd grow up happy and loved and maybe even marry one of the Miller boys.

She'd been as innocent as that baby. Had no idea what pain and guilt even meant.

Sara pulled up in front of the house, shoved the gear shift in Park, and left the engine running. "Thanks for the ride."

"What do you mean? You're not going to stay, are you? This place is derelict. I might even have been to a party here."

She shrugged. "I'll figure it out. It belongs to me, I guess. I want to look around."

"Then I'll wait," he said. "You can't just— I mean, you don't have any food or anything."

Good point. She hadn't got that far in her thinking. So much for logic.

"That's nice of you. Come on. Bring Nathan and we'll have a look around."

The front door was locked, so some enterprising party animal had broken the window out of the kitchen door and unlocked the back. And then no one had ever unlocked the front. Plenty of things had got in, though, besides people. Rain. Snow. Squirrels. Rats. Beer cans by the dozen lay all over. From here she could see into the sitting room, where the sofa was sprung and torn, but still sat where it always had. A couple of chairs she didn't recognize flanked it. She walked through and looked around. Two lamps black with soot sat on the floor. *Mamm*'s engagement clock, of course, was gone from the *Eck* cabinet, as were all her good dishes. The bookshelves were empty of all *Dat*'s books. But the floors were still sound, and none of the other windows were broken.

"I expected it to be completely trashed." She came back

into the kitchen and set her backpack on the table *Grossdaadi* had made her parents for a wedding present. Someone had carved their initials in it and the year—2019. "They could have used this table to feed the woodstove."

"Who would come out here in the winter?" He set the basket on the table next to her pack. The blanket wiggled and a muffled wail came from under it. "Aw, man, are you hungry again?"

She peered in as he pulled the blanket away. The red-faced months-old scrap of humanity in the blue knitted cap took one look at her and began to scream. "He's probably wet. I don't suppose the mother put an extra diaper in here?"

"I don't know."

"Well, you have a look while I go upstairs."

"Wait—"

But she didn't. The baby was his lookout, this poor old house was hers. She could hear Nathan screeching all the way up the staircase. Clots of mud lay on the hall floor. There was still a bed in one of the bedrooms, and the mattress and box spring, too, but not so much as a sheet on them. She'd have to get rid of them—it made her shudder to think what had gone on there. The other bedrooms were empty.

She stood in the doorway of her old room. It still smelled the same. Just a suggestion of pine and the faintest whiff of baby powder. She looked on the back of the door. Two hooks, one for each of her two dresses.

Shaking her head, she went back downstairs and into the bathroom. Water, miraculously, came out of the tap. Just a dribble, hardly any water pressure. Something must be gumming up the gravity feed from up the hill. The medicine cabinet was cleaned out and hung by one nail, as though someone had tried to take it, too, and given up halfway through the job. She hooked it on the other nail so it hung straight.

In the kitchen, the noise only seemed to have gotten louder. Nathan was lying on the table while Josh hunted through the basket.

"For Pete's sake, you idiot, never leave a baby like that." She picked him up and held him against her chest, her hand going to cradle his head by instinct. His whole body shook with sobs. "Poor little guy. He could roll over and splat right on the floor."

Josh didn't answer. Instead, he pulled out a diaper like a magician pulled a rabbit out of a hat. "Look. The basket is lined with these. Makes it soft, I guess."

Sara laid Nathan on the table and unzipped the snow suit. The diaper was full and had soaked through his sleeper into the snow suit. A cloud of baby poop fragrance enveloped them.

"Great." Josh gagged and handed her the diaper.

"Not my kid." She stepped back.

"I don't know how. I'm the youngest. No siblings to practice on."

"Lamest excuse ever. Give me that."

It wasn't something you forgot, diapering a baby, though these were the kind that had sticky tabs to close them, not big old safety pins. There was nothing to clean him with, so she pulled off her scarf, wet half of it, and used the other half to dry him. "She might have put some baby wipes in, too."

"I'm just glad about the diapers." He looked revolted as he watched. "How often do you have to do this?"

"As often as he wets or poops. There." She did the snaps up

on the onesie and put Nathan back in the snow suit, where he stared up at her. "Hold him while I go have a look at the barn."

"I'll come with you." But he took the baby and held him the way she had, hand cradling his head.

He followed her out into the yard, where the snow had melted enough to give them a clear path to the barn. Which was empty, of course, except for a lot of desiccated cow and horse and chicken droppings. The tack room had been cleaned out.

A buggy sat just inside the door, its rails down. Not the family buggy.

"*Dat* was a harness maker," she said. "All his tools have probably been stolen."

"Probably."

She checked his workshop just in case. The benches were empty except for bird droppings. She opened the closet set into the wall, its door made to look like plank paneling, too. "Well, hey." The two big rolling tool boxes sat there, and when she opened the lid of the first one, the rows of his punches and pliers met her surprised gaze. "How about that. They left the only things that are really valuable."

"Better leave them here, then, if they haven't been discovered in what—five years?"

She closed the lid. Five years.

Nowhere near long enough to diminish the pain.

"I heard you were in the car that hit them."

What was he, judge and jury? She slammed the closet door so hard that dust puffed out of it. The noise frightened the baby and he started to cry.

She left his father to deal with him and stomped outside. *Mamm*'s orchard was overgrown and leafless, but at least it was still alive. She pushed through the tall grass and smelled rotted apples. Heaps of them, lying frozen and useless, just good for pigs. She leaned on the Pippin in the corner, breathing hard, as if someone had been chasing her.

Not someone. Something.

Memory.

3

JULY, FIVE YEARS AGO

NOTHING BEAT OUTWITTING *Dat* and getting away. He'd forbidden her to go to this party, which he should have known would only make her want to go even more. She'd climbed out her bedroom window and now she didn't have to go to the bishop's for supper just to listen to the next thing to Sunday preaching for three solid hours.

The dangers of the world, Sara.

Rumspringe is for experimenting, not going all in and getting drunk every night, Sara.

Your family loves you, Sara. Some day every minute will be precious, and you'll wish you had back this time you're throwing away.

Bishop "Little Joe" Wengerd had been newly anointed, and stammered during his preaching. He thought he was doing his best, but he'd have done better just to be quiet. So would *Dat*.

She and two other Amish girls hooked up with two boys from California after a couple of drinks at Talley's. The boys wanted to go swimming, but didn't know the way to the lake. It was going to be so much fun. They had beer in the trunk and maybe they'd have trunks on. Or maybe not. She giggled to herself, squashed up against the driver as they flew down the road.

She squinted at the speedometer. Did that really say 100?

"County highway's the next one," she told him. "Stop sign. Left turn."

"How far?"

But she didn't know. All her landmarks were hidden in the dark, and they were going so fast that the whole world seemed to be scrolling by like a movie.

She liked movies. She—

Horse—lights—

"Stop!" she shrieked.

The car barreled through the stop sign and walloped the buggy in the intersection. The crash was deafening. In the headlights, she saw disjointed pieces, unable to make sense of them. The buggy flying—the horses dragged off their feet—a blanket—

"Stop!" she screamed again as the boy spun the wheel and gunned the engine down the county highway. The two girls with her were in hysterics.

A buggy! Who was it? Who?

He slammed on the brakes and she landed on the floor in a heap. "If you're just going to scream, get out." He leaned across to open the door.

"Go back! Help them!"

"Out!"

The three of them tumbled out into the weeds on the shoulder, staggering, trying to find their feet. Disoriented. In shock. Somebody gave them a lift home. She had no idea who.

And when she let herself in to the farmhouse, she was as quiet as could be. *Mamm* had ears like a cat. She passed out fully dressed on her bed, and slept like the dead until the next morning. The unfamiliar sound of rubber tires crunching on gravel woke her.

The house was still silent.

Until she opened the door.

"Is this the Fischer place, miss?" the policeman standing on the porch asked. A black and white state patrol car was parked in the gravel.

"Yes. I'm Sara Fischer."

He looked down at the Stetson he was turning around and around in his hands.

And then he told her there had been a hit and run.

Her nine-month-old little sister had lasted until daylight, and then died, too.

No survivors.

Present day

"Sara?"

She didn't turn around. Just looked up through the bare, gnarly branches at the sky. It must be close to midday by now, and her stomach felt so hollow it was probably sticking to her backbone. She couldn't remember when she'd finished the last granola bar. Coeur d'Alene, maybe? Had that been yesterday?

"I'm sorry. That was a stupid thing to say."

With a sigh, she turned. Josh stood there, awkwardly holding the baby against his shoulder, holding his head with its little blue cap.

"It's nothing more than the truth," she said at last.

"Still." The wind blew through the silence. "Look, you can't stay out here."

"I'll be fine."

He shook his head. "Fine means a cupboard full of food

and a pile of wood split for the stove. The Chinook won't last forever. It's going to freeze."

"You think?" She eyed the sky. The wind was almost warm.

"I know. I'm the guy breaking the ice on the cattle troughs at five in the morning."

"I can make do for one night," she said. "Tomorrow I'll go into town and see about a job. If they'll front me my first check, I can buy some groceries." She glanced back at the barn. "Hack up a milking pen for firewood if I can find the axe."

He was already shaking his head. "How about you come home with me? There's a ton of food in the house and a spare room. I've got to figure out this—" He looked down at Nathan. "—and you've got to figure out your next move, but neither of us can do it out here."

She hated it when strange guys thought they knew her business.

She hated it more when they were right.

The truth was, she didn't want to stay out here any more than he probably wanted that baby. But both of them had to face what the past had dealt them. The only difference was that she could walk away.

"All right," she said. "But only if your folks say it's okay."

He gazed at her. "Trust me, they're not even going to notice you."

He frowned down at the baby, which was good, because then he couldn't see Sara trying not to cry.

❦

"WHAT IN THE WORLD?" REUBEN SAID, THE REINS GOING slack in his hands.

Naomi Miller recognized the *Englisch* car instantly and her stomach, which had been more reliable lately, turned over with a sickening roll. "We've got company, I guess."

It was just the two of them in the buggy. Daniel was out in Whinburg Township with their cousins, Melvin and Carrie Miller and their family, helping Lovina Lapp and her sweet son Joel with the final preparations for their move out here. After years of separation and misunderstanding, they weren't wasting any time—he and Lovina would be married at the end of February. The twins, Malena and Rebecca, had stayed at Burk-holders' for the singing, as had Adam and Zach. And Joshua ...

Naomi swallowed and glanced at her husband. Either Joshua had driven himself here in that car, or his friend Tyler was dropping him off. Either way, her easy journey home with her husband, full of plans and hope and laughter, was about to come to an abrupt halt.

"Help me with the horse?" Reuben's voice was gruff.

"Of course." He didn't want her to go in the house alone, that was clear.

In the barn, they unhitched Hester, the buggy horse, and gave her a good rubdown and some extra oats for going the extra mile. Burkholders' was the last place in the Siksika Valley before the mountains rose in earnest, and it was a long drive. Then, with a glance at one another, they crossed the yard and went in the back door to the kitchen.

An *Englisch* girl with short dark hair sat at the table, putting away the leftover scrapple from this morning's break-fast, along with bacon and eggs, as though she hadn't seen food in days. Joshua sat opposite her with a baby in his lap, trying to feed it with a bottle at the same time as he forked food into his own mouth.

Joshua? Feeding an *Englisch* girl's baby?

Behind her, she felt the breath go out of Reuben as though someone had shoved him hard in the stomach.

Naomi had forgotten how to speak.

Fortunately, Reuben, who hoarded his words, had a few extra to lend. "Joshua? What is happening here?"

Their youngest looked up. *"Dat. Mamm.* Aren't you home early?"

"Neh. Who is this?" Reuben paused. "These?"

"It's a really long story," he said with a sigh. "But this is Sara Fischer."

"Sara—" Naomi's throat closed on the girl's name.

Everyone in the *Gmee* knew who Sara Fischer was. No one had heard from or of her in years. Some thought she must be dead. And now here she was at the Miller kitchen table, eating scrapple? Naomi would never have recognized that laughing rebel of a girl, her loose hair flying in the wind as she rode her father's buggy horse bareback, in this gaunt young woman. That hair was now cut shorter than an Amish boy's. Why was she wearing an Amish dress a couple of sizes too small?

Naomi tried again. "And this is Sara's *Boppli*? What is his name?"

The baby finished the bottle and Joshua gave up on his bacon and eggs. He held him against his chest and patted his back.

Naomi started forward. "Joshua, *neh,* you need to—"

The baby burped up all over Joshua's shirt in a cascade of milky fluid. The back of his onesie was stained and damp, and even from the door, Naomi could smell his diaper.

Her stomach turned over again. She must have made a noise, because Reuben slipped an arm around her waist. "Sit down, *Liewi.*"

"The baby's not mine," Sara said, scraping up the last of the egg yolk on her plate. "He's Joshua's."

Now it was Reuben's turn to gape speechlessly at their son.

"How is this possible?" Naomi said. Her voice sounded high and thready, even in her own ears.

Joshua reached into the wicker basket sitting on the table and took out an envelope. "Here."

Naomi read the letter inside it and passed it to Reuben. Then the birth certificate.

"Nathan Joshua Miller." Reuben looked up. "It's a good name. My *Daadi*'s name was Nathan."

"I don't understand," Naomi said. None of this made sense. "When did this girl give you her baby?"

"This morning. I was at the Rocking Diamond and when I got home, he was in the boot room in that." He tilted his head toward the basket while he dabbed unsuccessfully at his shirt. "I went to town and ran into Sara. Took her out to the Fischer place. She was going to stay, but the house is derelict and it's going to freeze tonight, probably. So we came back here to wait for you."

"You came in that car?" Reuben said.

"I still have my driver's license," Sara said. "I drove."

"Wait for us?" Naomi was having a hard time keeping up.

"*Ja.*" Joshua sounded as though this was the most reasonable thing in the world. "To help me figure out what to do with the baby."

Naomi stared at him. Her son. Who had fathered a baby he hadn't known about until this morning. She must not be sick. That was the one thing she could grab hold of in this particular minute. She must not be sick.

"There is nothing to figure out," Reuben said at last. "This girl of yours has abandoned her child. You are his father. You must raise your son."

Joshua's face lost its color. "I can't raise a child. And she's not my girl. She's just someone I spent a night with."

Reuben stiffened and grief at those hard, careless words forced a keening sound out of Naomi's throat.

"Your parents are right," Sara said. "Your one-night stand is long gone. Nathan's completely helpless. You're his father, no getting around that. Someone in his life has to do right by him."

"Says you," Joshua shot back. "You stay out of this."

"Don't speak to her that way," Reuben snapped.

"Why not? You know who she is, right?"

Reuben's glare sizzled the air between them. "She is Sara, and your guest. So you will do the right thing by both her and your son, and begin by treating them with respect and care."

"Oh, the way you treat me?"

"Joshua," Naomi moaned.

"Shut up, Josh," Sara said, sipping her coffee. "Picking a fight with your parents when you need them right now isn't very smart."

"Oh yeah? Well, at least I didn't—" His mouth closed with a snap.

Naomi stared at her son, appalled that he had nearly said such a terrible, wounding thing to a young woman who had already been so horribly wounded. What had gone so wrong in his spirit that he was so hateful? So bitter?

But in the next moment, she realized why he was doing it. He was lashing out, pushing away the people closest to him.

So they would not see his shame.

She could feel Reuben's body heat increase, and he shifted from foot to foot. In a moment he would lose his temper, which only happened about once a decade. She must not allow that to happen, or she would lose her son. The knowledge settled in her heart with certainty. Joshua would leave in that car and she would never see him again.

She rose from her chair at the table. "Joshua, *kumm mit*. We will get you and the little one cleaned up, and I will show you how to burp him so that it doesn't get all over you. Then we'll look out your old crib and some baby clothes. He can't spend another minute in these ones until they're washed."

"And then what?" he ground out, unwilling to give in.

"And then he will stop crying, and be comfortable, and you will have learned how to make him so."

There was no getting around mother logic. Without another word, Joshua collected the baby's things and put them in the basket, then followed her over to the sink. She undressed him and for the first time, held her grandson. His skin was so soft, and once he was clean, she would smell that delicious baby smell once again.

She hadn't realized until now that she'd missed it.

With gentle hands, she showed Joshua how to bathe Nathan and put him in another diaper. How to wrap him in a towel so he felt snug and secure. How to hold him until he fell asleep.

And the silence of a baby whose needs had all been met flowed into the kitchen like relief.

4

Joshua put the swaddled baby back in the basket and followed his mother downstairs to help her find the baby things. Sara had no idea what to say to the ropy, unsmiling man who leaned over the basket to gaze at his grandson. Looking for a family resemblance? She didn't have the courage to ask him about the spare room, so she did what would have been expected of her had she been at home.

Old habits died hard. Even in Portland, she'd kept her little place above the garage clean. She was always the one doing the dishes at the firehouse while the other EMTs kicked back after supper. But she hadn't minded. She liked order.

She got up and cleared the table, scraping the remains of Josh's breakfast into the bucket under the sink for the chickens. *Mamm* had had just such a bucket in exactly the same place.

When she got out the drain rack and ran hot water into the sink, Reuben Miller seemed to come to himself and realize what she was doing.

"You don't have to do that, Sara."

"It needs to be done."

"Then I'll help you."

Surprised, she watched him pull a dish towel off the handle of the propane stove as though he'd done it a hundred times before. Her father could make a pot of coffee, and knew what drawer the knives were in, but no more than that. The kitchen had been her mother's domain.

"So you've been out to the old place?" he asked, picking a coffee mug out of the drain rack and beginning to dry it.

"*Ja.* It was in better shape than I thought. No water pressure, though. Or hardly any."

"Not surprising. There's a year's worth of mud and dead leaves in the spring house, likely. I see you're dressed Amish."

"I plan to stay. To join church. Eventually."

He nodded. "That warms my heart."

A tingle of shock at such openness ran through her. She was nothing to this tough, middle-aged rancher. How could there be anything warm in his heart for her after what she'd done?

"I need to make amends," she mumbled.

He nodded, and started on the plates. "But going before the church can wait until you've had a chance to get your feet under you."

"Going before the church? You mean going to church?"

"*Neh, Maedel.* You'll need to ask forgiveness before the church, I expect. Little Joe will know more about that."

Her mind spun away from that subject as though it were an elk in the road. "I wondered why there was no one in the old place. I figured it would have been sold for back taxes."

Reuben glanced at her from under brows beginning to go gray. "It would have, but the church stepped in and paid them.

And then for a while, Rose from the quilt shop and her family were living there until they could buy their own place."

"Oh." She revised the history of the house in her mind. "So kids haven't been using it for a party house for as long as I thought."

"We tried to keep an eye on it, but everyone is busy."

"No, I'm just surprised. That the church would do that."

"No sense a good hay farm passing out of Amish hands," he said. "We kept the taxes paid up through a collection every year. Kept it in repair as best we could. Tried to rent it when we could. And we always hoped a family member—or you—might come back to make it a home again."

She turned back to the dishes. "Well, I did," she mumbled.

Going before the church. She wasn't sure what that entailed, but it couldn't be good. And yet, look what the *Gmee* had done. They didn't have to save her home on the odd chance she might come back. Then again, she supposed as the last remaining member of the family, she would have the title to it. Like Reuben said, they'd kept it in Amish hands.

Her hands, now.

Naomi and Joshua came upstairs from the basement, their arms full. "Look what we have here," Naomi said cheerily. "A crib, and lots of clothes, and there's even a dresser down there with a top for a changing table. I never gave them away after Joshua was born, though maybe as time went on, I should have. But I'm glad now I didn't."

She looked around the kitchen. Reuben hung up the towel while Sara wiped down the counters. "You've cleaned up?"

"*Ja,* it was the least I could do," Sara said. "It was the first meal I've had in a ... while."

"Well, it won't be your last." Naomi put the tiny clothes in neat piles on the table. "I hope you'll stay for supper, and the night. What are your plans?"

"I need a job, first," she said. "Thanks for the offer. I'll take it. Then I guess I'll find somewhere a little more permanent until I can save up enough to make the home place liveable again."

"She can stay here for more than a night, can't she, *Mamm?*" Joshua asked, sorting through the piles. "Does this little mattress go in the bottom of the crib?"

"*Ja*, with the mattress cover on, and that little blanket."

"Of course she can," Reuben said, and Sara breathed again.

"And as far as a job, I've got a good idea." Joshua made up the crib neatly, which surprised Sara a little. She'd pegged him for a more careless person. He turned to her. "Why don't you stay and look after the baby?"

Sara stared at him. Hadn't his father just told him *he* was going to be looking after his own baby?

Joshua lifted his shoulders as though everything were completely obvious. "It's the perfect solution. You live here and look after Nathan while I'm out doing ranch work."

"There is only one problem," Reuben said.

"Two problems," Sara corrected him.

"What?" Joshua looked from one to the other.

"One, I believe we already said that this baby is yours to raise. Not Sara's. Not your mother's. Yours."

"But *Dat*—"

"And two," Sara interrupted, "If I'm going to live at the farm, I'm going to need money. Being nanny to your kid for board and room might have worked in *Jane Eyre*, but even she got thirty pounds a year. Are you able to pay me the going rate for a nanny?"

Now it was the men's turn to stare. Naomi chuckled. "I liked that book."

"What *is* the going rate for a nanny?" Josh asked.

"I'd look it up on my phone, but it died in Coeur d'Alene," she told him dryly. "The point is, your parents are very kind to invite me to stay. If I could just bunk here until I find a job. Hopefully just a few days. Then I'll be out of your hair."

He turned to Naomi. "*Mamm*..."

But she only shook her head. "You heard your father. Nathan is yours to look after, like thousands of fathers before you have looked after their children."

"But what about the chores?" From his tone, you'd think they were all that mattered. And yet Sara had found him in a bar on Sunday morning. This morning. Good grief, was it still only Sunday?

Naomi leveled one of those looks at him that Sara's mother had directed at her all too often. "When Daniel was born, who do you think helped your father run the ranch after your uncles moved away?"

"*Daadi,*" Josh answered.

"*Ja,* sure, and *Mammi* ... and me. Because there was no one else. And yet somehow I managed to do my share of the ranch work, keep house, cook, and raise five more children. How did that happen, I wonder?"

Silence. Sara could swear she'd just seen Reuben smiling, but he was rubbing his hand over his mouth, so she couldn't be sure.

Joshua just stared into the basket with an expression that Sara couldn't quite read. Dismay, maybe? The look you got when someone locked the only door to your room—the one you'd been planning to leave by.

"Babies do best when they're on a schedule," *Mamm* went

on as if he'd agreed with her completely. "When he's hungry or needs to be changed, he'll cry to let you know. He'll need to sleep a lot. I won't expect you to carry him around in a sling while you're riding fence or working in the barn, though I had to. Between me and your sisters, someone will be here while he sleeps, and we can feed and change him if you're out with the cattle. But when you're close, I'll expect you to come in and deal with whatever he needs."

"But *Mamm*, I can't just drop everything to run in the house when he cries," Josh protested. "How will I get anything done?"

"This is a question many a young mother has asked herself," she mused, nodding. "You'll figure it out in time. Life will take on a rhythm that revolves around him. You'll be surprised how quickly you get used to it."

"*Mamm*, please—I'll do Rebecca and Malena's chores, too, if you'll just ask them to take care of—"

"If they had gotten themselves in *der familye weg*, I would be telling them exactly the same things." Naomi never raised her voice, its tone pleasant and warm and conversational. And implacable. "But they haven't. You have. In a manner of speaking."

"You're Nathan's father," Reuben said gently. "He will have love and attention and care from all his family. We will not desert him or you, and we will help you all we can. But he will learn the most of love at your hands, and give his first smile to you. Take his first steps with you holding him up. You will be the most important person in his life."

Joshua's face had gone pale and he looked almost sick.

"You will be a *wunderbaar* father," Naomi told her son. Love infused every word. "And he will grow up to love you like no one else, the way God's children love Him." She touched his shoulder. "Now, you must move the changing table into the downstairs spare room, and the crib. You'll want to be close to the kitchen so you can prepare his bottles during night feedings. Adam and Zach can bunk together, and Daniel will move down to his own house when he gets home, leaving his old room free for Lovina and Joel, as before. That leaves the little room above you for Sara."

"We'll do that now, while the boy is sleeping." Reuben rose from his chair. "Sara, maybe you wouldn't mind watching him?"

"Not at all," she said. "Let me know when I can help you with dinner, Naomi."

Naomi eyed her. "Are these your only clothes?"

"My only Amish clothes."

She nodded. "I'll see what I can find for you, too. You're taller than the twins, so Malena can sew you a dress that fits properly this week. She's very handy with a sewing machine, and between the two of you, you can make a dress in a day. But I can find you a cape and a *Duchly* for now, until we can ask Annie Gingerich to make you some *Kapps*. She earns a little money doing that for the women here."

"She did when I lived here before," Sara said softly. "Thank you, Naomi. I don't deserve—"

"The kindness you should have been shown before?" Naomi gazed at her. "I believe that every one of the *Gmee* ought to be asking *der Herr* for forgiveness. When you needed us most, it seems we drove you away."

Her mouth firmed and she climbed the stairs while her menfolk went down to the basement to bring up the dresser.

Except for the sleeping baby, Sara found herself alone. She was used to that. But for the first time in a long time, the loneliness that had been her constant companion was gone.

꧁ 5 ꧂

TRAPPED. He was trapped like a rabbit in a snare and if he didn't figure this out, he was never going to get away.

Joshua helped his father carry the chest of drawers upstairs. He moved out of his room and changed the sheets for Sara. He did everything *Dat* asked him to. And when the rest of his siblings came home, he did his best to ignore the girls' squealing and cooing and his brothers' barely concealed disgust as he showed them all Carey's letter.

But inside, under a face as calm as he could make it, he was a seething volcano of rage and resentment. If he could get his hands on Carey Lindholm for just two seconds... But of course he couldn't. She'd chosen her moment well, on a Sunday morning when she must have remembered there was an even chance an Amish family wouldn't be home. When the weather warmed up. When she could be reasonably certain that Nathan would be safe enough.

She'd probably had a getaway car waiting, and off she'd gone, as carefree as he had always dreamed of being. He barely remembered her, but he'd never forget her now, or forgive her for stealing his dream for herself.

He would figure this out. He had to. He was not going to lose Seattle, where the ocean was close and where it hardly ever snowed. Where there was lots of work and there were people strolling along the waterfront and going to music shows and where no one would ever look at him the way his brothers were looking at him now.

Joshua, the black sheep of the family. Joshua, the baby. Joshua, who was never satisfied with what he had.

In all the hubbub, Sara Fischer got off easy. The fact that she would be staying with them for a couple of days was completely overshadowed by the baby's arrival, just as he'd predicted.

He resented her, too. How come some people could commit the worst sins in the world, and yet people bent over backward to help them? Nobody was helping him. Nobody ever helped him, and now here he was with a baby like a boat anchor around his neck.

He couldn't live like this.

Could. Not.

Joshua spent a restless night, trying on one plan after another. The restlessness was compounded by the baby, who cried every twenty minutes, it seemed like, and needed to be fed. *Mamm* had showed him how to heat up the bottle in warm water, how to hold the baby properly, how to burp him. There were only two bottles left in the fridge. Maybe that was what stopped Joshua's brain from spinning out of control and presented him with the obvious solution.

He was in the kitchen, burping the baby like the best father in the world, when *Dat* came down at five a.m. to build up the fire in the woodstove. *Dat*'s quiet smile made him feel like a hypocrite, but that wasn't going to stop him.

After morning prayers, and breakfast, and seeing to the cattle, he said to Sara, "I have to take the car back to Tyler. Want a lift into town to start the job hunt?"

"*Denki,*" she said. "If Nathan is coming, you'd better go to the variety store and see if they have a car seat."

"Nathan isn't coming. *Mamm*, can you and the girls watch him while I take Sara into town?"

"How are you going to get home if you leave the car there?" *Mamm* was cuddling the baby and dropping kisses all over his little hands.

Well, shoot.

"I guess ... I'll take the buggy and Sara can drive the car over to Tyler's."

"The sooner it's out of your father's sight, the better," *Mamm* agreed. "We'll need baby formula today. You can get that at the drugstore. Don't bother getting more of these *Englisch* diapers. We found lots of cloth ones in the changing table. I thought I'd given them away, but I guess I didn't."

"Anything else?" As long as she didn't say *Take Nathan with you*, he could handle it ...

"Nathan has had a rough time," she went on. "I don't think he needs to go with you, or to be out and about any more than necessary. He needs quiet and safety and stability, because goodness knows what his little life has been like so far. Your sisters and I will look after him, but I want you home by noon. He'll have finished the last bottle by then."

"*Ja, Mamm.* I'll be at the drugstore when the doors open."

Luckily, neither *Mamm* nor his sisters asked why he was leaving so early if the drugstore didn't open until ten. But Sara did, as he was harnessing the horse.

"It's only three miles to town, isn't it?" she said, leaning on the side of the buggy as he backed Hester between the rails. "You got something else on the agenda?"

"You don't have to come," he said. "I can drive the car and you take the buggy."

"I have had way more experience driving cars than buggies lately. I don't mind dropping it off at your friend's. But what's up?"

She might be his second least favorite person right now, but if anybody would understand, it would be someone he wasn't related to. "I'm going to talk to Carey's parents."

A pleat formed between her brows. "What for? Seems like the whole baby issue is done and dusted."

"But it's not. They don't even know they have a grandson. What if they want him?"

She stared at him for so long that Hester shifted and gave a snort, as if to say, *Can we get moving?* "You're kidding me," Sara said at last. "He's your kid, not a volleyball, to get bumped and volleyed from one person to the next until he goes out of bounds."

Out of bounds. The place he most wanted to be.

He finished harnessing the horse, the job so familiar he hardly needed to pay attention while the possibilities filled his mind. "I think they deserve to know."

"Have you thought for one second what that will do to their relationship with their daughter?"

"Not my problem. She should have thought of that before she had a baby without telling them."

"They might not believe you."

He patted his pocket. "I'm taking her letter and the birth certificate."

With a sigh, she said, "Of course you are. Well, let's get moving, then, and get it over with."

"Like I said, you don't have to come."

"Someone has to make sure you don't bleed all over the buggy seat after her dad gets done with you."

Which wasn't the most encouraging thing she could have said. They agreed to meet at the *Englisch* elementary school, because the Lindholms lived one street over. He couldn't remember the house number, but he did remember the house. It was the only one in Mountain Home that had a sculpture of an eagle pouncing on a salmon in the front yard.

"Scary," Sara remarked as she got out of the buggy.

"Her mom is a sculptor. That's bronze."

"You had time to find this out during your one-night stand?"

"I learned about it later. From the girls who were her friends."

It was only half past eight when they knocked on the door, on which was a fat wreath studded all over with gold and silver balls. It was nearly Christmas and the sun was taking its time about coming up. There had been nowhere to tie up the horse, so they had looped the reins over the bumper of the car sitting at the curb.

A woman opened the door, dressed in a housecoat, her hair as short as Sara's. She took in the two of them, then the buggy. Her eyebrows went up. "Can I help you?"

"Mrs Lindholm?" Josh asked.

"Yes. Are you collecting for something? Isn't it kind of early?"

"No." Josh gave her his best smile. "I'm a friend of Carey's and I wondered if I could speak to you for a minute."

"Aren't you Amish?" Good question, he supposed. How

many *Englisch* kids had Amish friends? She still had one hand on the door, wavering as though she wanted to close it.

"Yes, but we got to be good friends. I'm Joshua Miller, and this is Sara Fischer. Could we come in?"

"Christine, who's at the door?" a man called from the back of the house. "The draft is coming in."

She turned her head. "A couple of Amish kids. Friends of Carey's."

"Well, tell them to come in. We're not heating the whole neighborhood."

She stood aside, and they followed her back through the house to the kitchen, where the man who had to be Carey's dad was eating breakfast. Joshua introduced them again.

"You know she's not home, right?" Mrs Lindholm said, leaning a hip on the counter. "She's gone to the U of M."

"Yes, I know," Josh said. "This isn't really about her, though." He fished Carey's letter and the birth certificate out of his pocket.

"What's that?" Mr Lindholm reached for it. Josh figured that Carey could do her own explaining, and handed it to him.

He read it through, while his wife read over his shoulder. She gasped, then backed away, a hand over her mouth.

"This has to be a fake." Mr Lindholm tossed it on the table, where Josh picked it up and tucked it back in his pocket. The other man was reading the birth certificate now. Then shook his head. "This, too." He glared at Josh. "Did you think you could just walk in here and ... what? Extort money out of us? You're disgusting."

"He's not extorting you, sir," Sara said. "You obviously know your daughter's handwriting. It's not a fake. But what you evidently don't know is ... your daughter."

"It's a lie," Carey's mother whispered. "Carey hasn't had a baby. She's been on an exchange term."

"You read what she wrote. She lied to you," Josh said.

"Or she did go away on her exchange, and had the baby there. Four months ago." Sara's voice was helpful. Pleasant.

Mr Lindholm leaped to his feet. "This is impossible. Do you know who I am? I'm an attorney, one of two in town, and if you don't want a libel lawsuit coming down on your head, you'd better not say that again."

"Slander," Sara said.

"What?"

"Libel is written. Slander is spoken. In any case, nobody is slandering anyone. We're just exchanging facts."

Lindholm turned scarlet and his mouth worked. While Josh admired her grit, he still wished Sara hadn't said that. No Amish girl would backtalk an *Englisch* man like that. Funny how she sounded more professional than he did.

"I just came to tell you that you have a grandson," he said as gently as he could, "and to ask if you'd like to get to know him. Maybe work out a—a—"

"Custody arrangement," Sara said.

"Cust—" Mr Lindholm looked as though he were about to have a heart attack. "Are you insane?"

"No," Josh said. "Nathan is at our place. If you'd like to see him, get to know him, maybe even have him for a while, I can go and get him."

"You *are* insane," Lindholm said, finally able to form a complete sentence. "Get out of my house."

"But he's your grandson," Sara protested. "Don't you even want to meet him?"

"I don't have a grandson," he snapped. "I have a son at UCLA and a daughter on a volleyball scholarship, and that is all. I don't know what your game is, but if I ever see you around here again, I'll have you arrested."

"It's not a game." Desperately, Josh took the birth certificate, stabbed the county seal with his finger. "This is real. The baby is real. I can't look after him. I've just turned twenty-one and I'm going to Seattle. You have to do the right thing, Mr Lindholm."

"The only thing I *have* to do is kick you two lunatics out of my home." He leaped to his feet and tore the breakfast napkin out of his pristine white shirt collar. His face was as red as the discreet pattern in his tie. "Out. Now, before I call the police."

"But—"

Sara grabbed his sleeve. *"Kumm mit,* Josh. We've got our answer. Let's go."

And there was nothing he could do but stuff the birth certificate back in his pocket and follow her out at a fast walk. As they went down the steps, the front door slammed so hard the big wreath fell off and rolled into the shrubbery. Hester jerked as though she'd heard a rifle go off, and it took him a minute to calm her while Sara untied the reins.

As he flapped them over Hester's back and she took off at a trot, Sara looked over her shoulder. Then she chuckled.

"What?" he said. "What can you find so funny right now?"

"Hester," she told him, a grin on her face. It was the first time she'd smiled a real smile since he'd met her yesterday. "She left a nice big present for the Lindholms, right behind their forty-thousand-dollar BMW."

She giggled about it every few minutes all the way to the drugstore. But his life was circling the drain, and Joshua just couldn't see his way far enough to crack a smile.

6

THE TOWN of Mountain Home came fully to life by midmorning, no doubt anxious to snag what few Christmas shoppers there were. Sara had to admit the place was kind of cheery, with its swinging signs on iron hangers above, beautiful window displays, and sandwich boards out on the sidewalk that encouraged the county highway traffic to slow down and consider stopping.

Surely someone would give her a job. Surely she'd have better luck at that simple task than poor Joshua had had with the Lindholms.

Sara tried at Yoder's Variety Store while Joshua was buying necessities for the baby, but it was a family outfit and they had two daughters over eighteen who had the place well in hand. She walked out with a *Kapp* that fit, though, at no charge. She thought maybe the girls' mother had recognized her and this was her way of doing something small to help. Her thanks were sincere as she fitted the bucket-shaped Montana *Kapp* designed to accommodate a bun over her short hair. At which point she discovered that straight pins didn't anchor the *Kapp* to short hair the way they did through hair drawn straight back and secured.

"Try this," one of the daughters whispered, and tore a strip of double-sided tape off a roll under the counter. She showed Sara where to put it inside the brim, and sure enough, its other sticky side adhered to her hair.

"Brilliant," she said with a grin. *"Denki."*

"We don't use it every day, just for Sundays and special. Mostly because it pulls at our hair when we take it off. Will you be staying?" the girl asked shyly. "We don't have so many *Youngie* here. It would be nice to have another girl."

"I'm staying at the Circle M until I get my feet under me," she said. "And I guess whether I'm staying for good depends on the bishop."

The girl nodded. "I hope you do."

There was another thing that needed to go on her to-do list. A meeting with the bishop. But there were more urgent errands today.

In the quilt shop, Rose Stolzfus shook her head regretfully and said that she didn't have an opening. "The shop is so tiny and between me, the bolts of fabric, and the quilts I sell on consignment, more than one person probably wouldn't fit. But you might try at the market," she said. "They always need help at this time of year."

But there, if the *Youngie* rolling carts out to the parking lot or stocking shelves were any indication, it appeared they had all the help they needed.

Sara continued down the road, asking in each shop regardless of what they made or sold. Alden Stolzfus, the young blacksmith, raised his eyebrows at her when she asked if he needed any help. When she suggested she might help in the front office, he shook his head and said his sister usually sat there, but she was at home because it was laundry day.

With the Amish shops exhausted, she turned to the *Englisch* ones. But there, too, she struck out. The college-aged kids were all home for Christmas, which gave them seasonal help. She wasn't sure if she wanted to work for an *Englisch* shop, anyhow. They tended to not understand about employees not working on Sunday, and if she was going to return to the church, that was not up for discussion.

Set back on a side street, she saw the shed and the county sign out front. The volunteer fire department. The engine was out in the driveway and a couple of volunteer firefighters were washing it down. She walked up to them and nodded politely when one of them wished her good morning.

"I've just come back to town and I'm looking for work," she said. "Any chance you have an opening for an EMT on your team?"

The man pushed up the bill of his cap with its silver Siksika VFD insignia. His sober but curious gaze took her in. "You certified?"

"Yes," she said. "CPR of course, and the NREMT. I just got recertified before I left the department I was with outside Portland."

"Driver's license?"

"Yes."

"But you're Amish."

That stopped her. She hadn't had a license when she left the fold five years ago. And it wasn't likely that *Ordnung* would have changed in those years, allowing her to keep the one she had. "Not at the moment."

He indicated the *Kapp* with his chin. "Wear that for fun, do you?"

She tilted her head from side to side, indicating a decision. "I used to be. I've been gone for five years, and now that I'm back, I'm probably going to be again. Is that a problem?"

The younger man shook his head and went back to polishing the engine with his rag, leaving the conversation up the shift captain.

"It's a problem if they make you give up your license. All of us are EMTs on the volunteer crew. All of us have to do our share, whether that's driving or dispatching or whatever. Not having a driver's license could mean you couldn't get to a car accident or a house fire."

"But I wouldn't be a firefighter." She waved a hand at her poorly fitting dress. "Just an EMT. I'd ride along, do dispatch, cook when it's my turn ... just not drive."

"Your desire to help out is commendable," he said. "And any one of us would be grateful for someone besides us to rattle the pans. There isn't a cook among any of these jokers on B shift."

"Hey," came from behind the rig. "I made bratwurst, didn't I?"

"But a driver's license is pretty much a prerequisite before we can even talk about a new recruit," the older man went on. "I'm sorry."

She thought fast. "I need a job so I can fix up the property my folks left me. Make the house livable. What about going out on calls where the victims are Amish? Could I help there, with translation as well as medical assistance?"

"Miss— What's your name?"

"I'm Sara. Sara Fischer."

He gazed at her. "You talking about the old Fischer place? The family killed in that accident?"

"Yes." Her throat closed up and she could say no more.

"I was on that call. Worst one of my life. I hope I never have to—" He turned away for a moment, hands on hips and head bowed, then cleared his throat. "The driver of that car got twenty-five years in prison. Homicide by vehicle with a DUI, plus a string of other charges."

Part of her felt a spurt of satisfaction. But it still wouldn't bring her family back, or lessen her guilt at not doing something—anything—to make him slow the car before it reached the intersection.

"I'm glad," she croaked.

"Thanks for the offer of help," he said. "With this job, as you know, it's typically all or nothing, but if you were a regular member of the team, we could use you. Send you to that Farm Rescue course. But if the church nixes the driver's license, my hands are tied."

She nodded. The church would indeed nix it. "I'm sorry, too," she said. "I would have liked to work here. Seems like a good crew."

"They are. Well, if you change your mind ..."

A rueful smile curved her mouth. "Not likely. But thanks. I do have a Plan B, so I'll give it another look."

"Take care, Sara Fischer."

"You too. Keep the wet stuff on the red stuff."

"Always."

Sara retraced her steps through Mountain Home's downtown and kept going on the county highway. She had no idea where Joshua was, but it didn't matter. She could walk three miles on a bright morning like this. Back to the Circle M.

Back to her pending employment as an abandoned baby's full-time nanny.

By the time he'd collected baby formula and wipes from the drugstore, and then a bag to carry supplies in, plus a couple of little onesies and sleepers from the Yoders at the variety store, Joshua was in a foul temper. So much for trying to save his money. So much for that nest egg he'd been growing so carefully, like some kind of rare plant that needed to be coddled. He resented every last cent represented by the stuff in the carrier bags in the back of the buggy.

Not only that, he knew the Yoder girls. The news of the baby would be all over the valley by suppertime, and there wasn't a single thing he could do about it.

He was a mile down the road leaving town when he recognized the slender, rangy figure in the too-short dress and the cowboy boots. That long stride that took her down the traffic side of the snow heaped up by the county blade. He whistled as he pulled up behind her, and she turned.

"I thought you'd be at home long before now." She went around the rear of the buggy, climbed in, and settled herself on the passenger side to his left.

"I'm in no hurry." With a flap of the reins, Hester moved out.

"Get everything?"

"Enough for now. How come babies are so expensive when they're so little?"

"We should have extorted some maintenance money from the Lindholms." When he was too surprised to reply, she said, "Joke. Sorry. My sense of humor is kind of dark."

"What about you? Any luck?"

She shook her head. "Nothing. Except that Della Yoder gave me this *Kapp*. That was something. I think she felt sorry for me. I even asked at the firehouse. If it wasn't for the

47

impending loss of my driver's license, they might have taken me on."

He turned his head, even more surprised. "The firehouse?" What were the odds of ever hearing *Kapp* and *firehouse* in the same breath?

"Yeah. I'm an EMT. I worked on a volunteer fire crew when I lived in Portland."

He'd have been astounded at a girl doing such a thing if that final fact hadn't overridden his good sense. "You lived in Portland?" he blurted. "That's only a few hours from—" He stopped himself just in time.

"From Seattle? I guess. Did I hear you say you were moving there when we were talking to the Lindholms?"

Stupid, stupid! "Yep. Don't tell my parents, okay?" He should never have said that with her in the room, but it had just jumped out. What was wrong with his mouth lately? He couldn't seem to control it.

She eyed him. "I'd say it was none of my business, but it appears that my only employment option around here is nannying your kid. So if you up and go to Seattle, where does that leave me?"

Honestly, if she were at the Circle M, she'd be in good hands and he'd be gone, guilt free.

She must have seen something in his face, because she shook her head. "Oh, no. No, you don't. You are not going to stick your family with your son and hightail it off to the coast. Don't even think about it."

The rage at the unfairness of his life surged up into his throat. "Don't tell me what to do," he growled.

"Oh. Right. Because your own self-control and good judgement are doing such a fine job so far."

He swore violently, and didn't realize he'd yanked on the

reins until Hester came to a confused stop in the mouth of someone's lane.

"Shut up," he said. "Just shut up."

"Okay." Which lasted for all of two seconds. "But somebody has to tell you the truth. Have you got five grand in your pocket?"

The audacity of the question actually made an answer fall out of his mouth. "No." He got Hester on the road again.

"Well, rent in Seattle is around a thousand a month for a bachelor suite—that means one room with maybe a hot plate and a toilet—out on the ragged edges of town. First and last month up front, plus security deposit, plus cleaning fee. That leaves you two grand to live on, provided you get a job within the first month."

No. That couldn't be true. She was making it sound worse than it was so he didn't do exactly what she'd accused him of.

She glanced at him. "Nobody ever told you that? Have you done any planning at all?"

"Of course I've been planning. For years. Tyler was going to go with me, so we'd have the car, but now he's going to work with his uncle at some moving company. So I'm going on my own."

"Well, if you take Nathan with you, you'd have to factor in child care, too, at six hundred a month."

He made a noise of protest, but she just kept going.

"At least I had a support network. I lucked on to an ex-Amish family through Facebook when I was eighteen, and they let me stay with them until I got my GED and passed my EMT certificate. Rafe was a volunteer fireman and I got lucky. You don't need a college degree for the EMT. I wanted to be a paramedic, but not bad enough to sacrifice another four years. I'm twenty-three now."

49

"Maybe there are ex-Amish in Seattle. Maybe I could do the same."

"Nathan might make that tricky. I mean, there probably isn't an Amish or ex-Amish woman alive who doesn't love babies. But you can't expect them to help you with child care for free."

His two thousand precious dollars wouldn't go very far if child care really was that expensive. And if he couldn't find the ex-Amish community, how would he find nice people to look after the baby in a population of hundreds of thousands? It had once seemed like paradise, to be absolutely unknown in a strange place, free to do and be whatever he wanted. But with a baby? The list of possibilities shortened right up.

He guided Hester into their lane and threw a glare in Sara's direction. "You had the perfect life," he said. "Why in the world would you come back?"

She huffed a laugh, gazing at the lane furling out between Hester's ears. The split rail fence and the cows beyond it in the home paddock. The mountains circling the valley that held him prisoner.

"Because it's the world," she said simply. "And this is home."

With a sigh, he pulled the horse to a stop in front of the house so she could carry his purchases inside. Then he led Hester into the barn. Just his luck to stumble over the one person in the world who had given up the very life he would give anything to have.

7

Sara honestly didn't think poor Nathan would survive his first week at his father's hands. EMT training didn't include psychology, but anyone could see that he resented every minute the baby took from him and, presumably, every dollar that wasn't going toward his flight to Seattle.

Naomi gazed at him with a combination of sorrow and confusion when he handled the child without gentleness. He got the job done—changing a diaper, feeding, burping—and then pushed out of the kitchen to return to whatever task he was working on. Cleaning tack seemed to be his particular job on the ranch outside of the regular winter maintenance work and feeding the cattle. Maybe the tack got cleaned to a shine so he didn't have to spend so much time with the baby. Sara didn't know. But she remembered her own father's care of the harness he made, his quiet satisfaction when his efforts with saddle soap and rag were done.

Josh wasn't showing much quiet satisfaction with anything.

"You need to show him he's loved," Naomi said on Thursday afternoon as Joshua awkwardly got Nathan back into his terrycloth sleeper. "Just spend a few minutes holding him, letting him know he's safe."

"Can't you do that?" Joshua wanted to know. "Or Sara?"

"We're not his father," Naomi said in the same gentle tone. "He needs to be attached to you. We're just the people around him. He's getting used to us, but actual attachment takes holding and attention and love that he can feel."

Josh sat in the rocker in the corner with the baby on his chest, patting his back while he watched the second hand on the kitchen clock over the door make exactly five sweeps. Then he carried him into his room, put him in his crib, and came out.

"I'll be in the barn mucking out the horses' stalls," he said.

"You'd rather do that than cuddle a baby?" Malena said in amazement, but the kitchen door had already closed behind him. The cold air let in by his departure dissipated in the warmth of the woodstove.

With a sigh, Naomi sat at the table where they had been enjoying coffee and oatmeal cookies jeweled with raisins, dried cranberries, and bits of citron peel. She bit into a cookie and wrapped one arm around her stomach.

"Are you okay?" Sara asked.

She nodded. "Just tired. And worried. Which is probably why my stomach is upset. I'm wondering if I should just mother that little scrap myself before he begins to think he doesn't have a parent at all."

"I've wondered if I should do the same thing," Sara confessed. "How do *Englisch* nannies keep from becoming attached to the kids they look after? I've met some parents that leave all the upbringing and cuddling and putting bandages on scrapes to the *au pair*, and see their kids every day just long enough to kiss them good night."

Naomi shuddered. "It sounds terrible. Joshua could never be like that."

"He just needs time to adjust." Rebecca sat next to Sara and reached for a cookie. "We've all been adjusting this week. It seems kind of hard for you and *Dat* to insist that Joshua come in and do the changing and stuff, though. Women were made to look after babies. We're right here in the house and could do it in a second."

"You know why, *Dochder*," Naomi said.

"To teach him a lesson about getting involved with *Englisch* girls," Malena said firmly, taking a second cookie.

At the moment, it was just teaching him to resent the poor baby, but Sara would never say so out loud. Surely he couldn't help falling in love with his son? Sara was half in love with him already, and she had never been the maternal type. At least, she'd never thought so. But he was so tiny and so cute, and had a way of looking up at you through sleepy eyes that just made you thankful you'd made him so content.

Because outside of the screaming welcome they'd got the day they'd brought the formula home—the bottles had run out and he was massively hungry—he seemed to be a happy little guy. But he wasn't very old, so it was probably too soon to tell what kind of personality he would have.

The sound of buggy wheels churning through the mud outside made Malena fly to the window over the sink. "My goodness," she said. "It's the bishop."

"He's heard about the baby," Naomi predicted, getting to her feet. "I'm glad he won't be greeted by screaming the moment he walks in, anyway. Rebecca, better make another pot of coffee. You know how he likes it."

Sara had a moment to be thankful that she was wearing a new green dress, cape, and apron that actually fit. Malena had chosen the color from her stash of fabric in her room, because she said it brought out the green in Sara's eyes. Yesterday they'd finished a blue one for Sundays, and had run up a black bib apron, too, while they were at it, for around the ranch.

She felt for the first time as though she could join in to welcome the bishop instead of cringing about her ill-fitting clothes from five years ago. That old purple dress had gone into Malena's scrap bin. Sara supposed that eventually she would see pieces of it in a quilt.

Little Joe and Sadie came in on another cold draft that told Sara the Chinook winds had changed their mind and they were back to winter. After a flurry of taking off coats and hats, they were invited to seat themselves at the table while Rebecca poured coffee and Malena offered a refreshed plate of cookies.

Little Joe Wengerd folded his six-foot-five length into a kitchen chair and accepted the coffee. "Just the right amount of cream, Rebecca," he said with a grin. "You know me well."

Rebecca blushed with the praise.

The bishop's gaze turned to Sara. "It's been many a year since I sat down with you, Sara Fischer. Welcome back to the Siksika."

She felt the heat in her own face. "I'm home for good, Bishop."

"I'm for sure and certain glad to hear that. You look well."

With a glance at Naomi, she said, "They're feeding me like they're trying to fatten me up."

"And here I thought I was being subtle," Naomi said with a smile.

"But are you well?" Joe persisted. "Well in your spirit? Your soul?"

"That's a little harder," Sara said cautiously. "I'm so grateful to the Millers for taking me in and giving me a job. I'm little Nathan's nanny."

Sadie wriggled as though she were dying to get words out. "We heard there was a baby in the house. May I see him?"

"Girls, let's take the bishop's wife in for a visit."

And as Naomi and the girls trooped into the baby's room with Sadie, Sara realized why Little Joe was here. "You and Sadie didn't come about Joshua and the baby, did you?"

He helped himself to a second cookie. "We came about whichever of you was home. I'm glad to talk to you, Sara. Please don't think I'm here to punish you, or to make you suffer any more than I'm pretty sure you already have."

"And still do," she whispered, taking a sip of coffee to hide the tears that sprang without warning into her eyes. "I miss them so much. It's worse since I've been back. Going to the farm was—" She stopped. Swallowed. "Hard."

Without a word, he leaned over to the kitchen counter and plucked a tissue out of the box there. Sara had a moment to wonder if he knew where the tissue boxes were in every home in the district before she nodded her thanks and blew her nose.

There. That was enough sniffling. She could do this.

"The *gut Gott* will be your comfort, Sara," he said gently. "He has held you in His hand and brought you back to us. I have prayed for this day."

She nodded. "So have I. I want to join church."

She sensed something loosen in him, and when she looked up, it was to see a man filled with joy. And he was a big man, so there was a lot of joy. "Then my prayers are answered."

"I want to live at the old place," she said hoarsely, "and pay back the taxes to the church, and take up my life again somehow."

He nodded. "But until all that is possible, you've found a refuge here. I'm glad. Maybe you'll..." His words faded as he gazed in the direction of the barn.

Maybe she would what? Be a good influence on Joshua? She wasn't about to tell him that was not likely to happen. Not with Seattle still in the picture, a prospect with a much greater allure than any woman.

The bishop's intense blue eyes, fanned with wrinkles at the corners from laughter and riding the range, held hers. That was the opening act. Here came the real reason for his visit.

"But before you can begin baptism classes, I'm afraid we have an unusual situation we must take care of."

She gazed at him, waiting. It couldn't be worse than what she'd been through already.

"I only know of one time where anything like this has happened. Where an individual had to come before the church for this reason. Normally we would wait until Council Meeting in the spring, when we all ask forgiveness of one another, but with your desire to be baptized before that, I feel it would be better done earlier, before you begin classes. Do you know why?"

"For the old life is passed away," she whispered, "and I will be made new." Her involvement in the accident, her flight from the valley in a storm of fear and rage when the truth had come out, courtesy of the other two girls who had been in the car, all washed away in the water of the Spirit and the blood of the Lamb.

Had those girls left, too? Or were they young wives now, having been baptized and forgiven?

"*Ja*, I see that you understand. In our year, baptism comes on New Life Sunday, before Council Meeting, when we would ask for and receive forgiveness. But I think it will be better this way. Forgiveness, and then everything washed away in your baptism. It will be hard, but it must be done so that there will be cleansing and, as you say, you can take up your life again."

She nodded. The order of events mattered less than—

"Forgiveness, Sara," Little Joe said as though he had read her thoughts. "You must forgive yourself for your part in what happened, and the church must forgive you. To do that, you must come before us on your knees."

To hear him say it, so gently, so inflexibly, made tears well in her eyes.

"I will give you the words, and you will repeat them after me. The *Gmee* will respond. I will pray over you, and as I do, I hope God will intercede and allow you to forgive yourself. And we will be able to welcome you into fellowship with gladness."

"And I can take classes after that?"

"*Ja*, they start at our home on January twenty-fourth."

When she was baptized on New Birth Sunday, she would commit her life to God and to this community. It was a promise she had come to with a sense of inevitability as the life she had been living became narrower and narrower until finally, there was only one choice.

To come back and take up the life God wanted for her.

She nodded again. "Would I start as soon as that?"

"When you are ready. There will be more classes leading up to Communion in the autumn."

She wanted to say *the sooner the better*, but didn't. The desire to do what was right was one thing, but if she'd learned anything as an EMT, it was that the minute you thought you were in control of your life, that was when *der Herr* would throw you a curveball.

"All right," she said. "I'll do it. After Christmas."

"Your willingness is like a blessing to me, Sara," he said.

"We have time to talk again, to prepare, this month yet. I wasn't sure what would happen if I spoke so soon after your coming home. If you would get angry and leave again, maybe. Or be so offended that you'd stay here and live *Englisch*, and we would see you every day in the town, like a bruise on my conscience that would never heal."

"I've had enough of that," she said, one corner of her mouth quirking up ruefully. "Anger and offense are great ... for a day. But living with them for a lifetime? *Neh, denki.*"

"A lot of folks can go many years without learning that," he said, his smile reflecting her own.

"A lot of folks probably haven't been through what I've been through. Which reminds me, Bishop ... I was an EMT out in Oregon. I drove the emergency medical van as part of my job. The shift captain here at the Siksika volunteer fire department said they could use me, but I needed to keep my license."

He gazed at her. "You are not baptized yet. You are free to use this license."

"We both know that's not really going to happen. If I'm planning to be baptized, I need to be preparing. Giving up the things of the world."

"Then why are you asking me?"

She knew what the answer would be to this one, too. But she had to ask. "To see if an exception can be made for me. Since I came with the license, in a way."

His face filled with the humor she remembered. Her little brother had once asked *Mamm* if the bishop was actually God, because of his booming voice and white beard. They had loved it when he and Sadie had come to visit. "I could make an exception for that," he said. "And I could make an exception for Joshua Miller's car. And I could make an exception for this, that, and the next thing and soon I wouldn't have to make exceptions. Because the *Gmee* would be doing just as it wanted, and they wouldn't even need me anymore."

He looked so comical at the prospect that she had to laugh. "All right. I get it. No license."

"But without it, you can still have a useful place with us. Because what you will still have is your EMT training."

"I have to take the certification classes every year to keep it up."

"There are Amishmen in other communities who are EMTs. Gordonville is one such, in Lancaster County. Life can be hard here, and skills like this useful to us and others. I will write to one of the bishops and ask about this certification. What it means to an Amish person to be bound by it." He gazed at her. "And here is another thing to consider. We have never had a *Dokterfraa* in Mountain Home. Perhaps this might also be a way for you to help your community and make your living as well."

She'd heard the word before, but never met one. "A *Dokterfraa?*"

"*Ja.* An herbal healer."

A voice spoke from behind them. "My husband's cousin says they have a skilled *Dokterfraa* in Whinburg Township. Sarah Byler." Naomi Miller led Sadie and the two girls back into the kitchen. Sara had been so astonished by the *Dokterfraa* idea she hadn't even heard them. Sadie was cuddling little Nathan against her chest, and he yawned a huge yawn. Malena filled a pot with water and turned on the burner to warm a bottle of formula. "Carrie Miller could put you in touch with her."

Sara's mouth closed with difficulty as she tried to sort

through her feelings. "I—I've never even seen a *Dokterfraa*. I don't know what she would do."

"Perhaps this Sarah Byler could tell you what might be involved. And then you would have what you need to decide," Sadie said. "Don't let my husband railroad you into doing something you don't want to, mind. I know how he is."

"It was just an idea, *Fraa*," he said. "Did you know that Sara here is an EMT?"

"I didn't," Sadie said. "But how *wunderbaar*, to have an EMT among us."

The words were barely out of her mouth when the baby realized he was not being held by someone he knew. He wriggled and let out a yell. Naomi took him and glanced at Malena, who tapped a few drops from the bottle on to her wrist.

"Almost warm," she said.

The bishop rose from his chair. "I will leave you good women to care for this lost little one who has been found," he said. "Is Joshua in the barn?"

"I hope so," Naomi said. "But Rebecca can run down and ask him to come up here."

"*Neh*, I'll go." He pulled his coat off the tree by the door. "The barn seems to be a good place to have a conversation. And if I don't see Joshua, I can always get good counsel from the horses."

ONE THING ABOUT RAGE—IT GOT THE WORK DONE TWICE AS fast as usual. While *Dat* and his brothers were out with the wagon, tossing hay to the cattle in the zigzag pattern that would re-seed the field naturally come spring, Joshua was mucking out stalls. And hoping to work off some of the anger he felt at the injustice of his situation.

Seattle. The baby. His family. His dreams and his reality seemed to be at the opposite ends of a long road, and he couldn't seem to find his way from one to the other. Not with his self respect intact. Or his bank account.

He'd finished the third stall and wheeled the manure outside to the compost pile when he saw the tall figure waiting for him on his return.

"Bishop," he said, nodding as he passed him.

Little Joe followed him in. "Need a hand?"

"*Neh*, I can do it."

"Never said you couldn't." The bishop got a shovel and took the next stall. The scrape of metal on concrete was the only sound for some minutes. Well, Joshua wasn't about to start the conversation the bishop clearly wanted. All he had to do was wait him out.

"Seems like a healthy *Boppli*, your boy," the older man said at last. His muscles bunched as the shovel swung in a regular rhythm.

Joshua didn't answer. His boy. Right.

"He has the look of you and your father. And maybe your brother Daniel. Around the forehead and chin."

He made a noise in his throat. "His mother says I'm the father. I guess the forehead and chin prove it."

"You don't believe her?"

"Whether I do or don't doesn't matter. He's here, and she's not."

"Where is she now? What is wrong with this girl, that she can leave her baby like this?"

"She's at university, I guess. She wants that, and not the baby."

Over the top of the stall, Josh saw him shake his head sadly. "Poor girl. She will be a stranger to him."

"No big loss."

"So you don't love her, this girl. You don't plan to marry her." Two statements, not two questions.

"Nope."

"What do you plan to do?"

He'd had a lot of plans. They would have carried him down that road from here to there. But now? His frustration boiled over. "What I want to know is, why does Carey Lindholm get to walk away from her responsibilities when I don't, Bishop? And don't tell me it's God's will. God has nothing to do with any of this."

The bishop was silent for nearly a minute, shoveling manure into the wheelbarrow. "I wonder. I suppose we will see. But what fills me with gratitude, Joshua, is that you are taking responsibility. A boy can't do that. Only a man can."

"Yeah, well..." Boy, man, what difference did it make?

"Nathan needs responsible men in his life, to show him what it means to be godly. Honorable. Humble. Useful. I am glad he has you for that."

"I don't think he does. None of that describes me at all."

"I don't know about you, but I feel both humble and useful right now. Manure tends to do that to a man."

Josh absolutely did not want to smile, but it happened anyway. "Two out of four isn't bad, I guess."

"Oh, I think all four are at work. Otherwise, you might have climbed into that car and driven away already with your *Englisch* friend."

Joshua's skin went cold. How did he know? How? Had Sara told him, up there in the kitchen? Was that why he was here?

"I just wanted you to know that the church is here for you

if you need us. Sadie and Ruby are only too happy to babysit. Sadie misses having babies in the house."

"Denki." That was the last thing he expected Little Joe to say. "Sara is helping, too."

"I don't know how she came into your household, but I'm very happy she did."

"It was kind of an accident. We bumped into each other in town and she had noplace else to go. Have you seen the state of the Fischer farm?"

"Ja, I go by there every week. I try to keep an eye on it, make sure vagrants don't move in."

Joshua stood the shovel up against the wall, turning away to disguise his surprise. "I was thinking I might go by again, make a list of things that need to be repaired. Like that window in the back door."

"Ja, that would be good. And the porch steps in the front could use a few new planks. Someone's going to go through them one of these days. Probably me."

"Seems like the springhouse is plugged up, too. Be good to get that running again."

"Maybe we men could organize a work day. I could probably squeeze some cash for parts and supplies out of the deacon if I broached the subject after dinner. I could ply him with some of Sadie's pecan pie."

Joshua nodded. "That would be *gut*. I'll go tomorrow, maybe."

"I don't know if Sara is serious about living there, but a few repairs could make it possible, at least. Maybe she'd like a renter to bring in some money."

"I don't think she's thought of that." Joshua hadn't, either. "It'd be hard for her to be a nanny here if she was living there, but if she had renters..."

"Lots of possibilities," Little Joe agreed. "We'll think on it, all of us." He put up the shovel and surveyed the cleaned stalls. "Guess I'd better be getting back to my wife. Nice talking with you, Joshua."

"And you, Bishop."

And strangely, it had been. He'd always seen the stern side of Little Joe Wengerd. The cattleman who did what needed to be done, whether that was doctoring his herd or counseling a wayward member of his flock. He'd never seen the ... well, the shepherd side of him. The thoughtful problem solver. Like *Dat*.

He'd thought he was going to be preached at, when instead he got a few ideas to help Sara. Well, that was better than nothing.

Because he doubted the bishop had any ideas about helping Joshua get to Seattle.

❧ 8 ❧

December 18

Dear Carrie,

By the time this letter reaches you and Melvin, it will be Christmas, so let me just share my joy with you and yours. Please give Daniel and Lovina and Joel a big hug from me and Reuben. Joel and your children will be looking forward to Christmas treats and seeing all the family—because goodness knows Christmas is a whole different season when there are children in the house, isn't it?

I have some strange and wonderful news to share. Joshua, my youngest, is apparently a father at twenty-one years of age! The mother of little Nathan Joshua Miller abandoned him practically on our front porch, and thank goodness we were having a Chinook or he would have frozen to death. The girls and I have fallen in love with him already, and while Joshua has some decisions to make, I hope and pray that the Lord will guide him to do what's right. He is very angry and conflicted right now, and needs his Lord's love more than ever.

Along with the baby, a nanny appeared on the very same day. Actually we're all nannying this little treasure, but Sara Fischer has returned to the Siksika, and she is staying with us for now. She told us at supper last night that the bishop has made the way plain for her to be baptized in the spring, so it was a real celebration. You remember when I wrote to tell you of her family, killed so tragically a few years ago. She was with some Englisch boys and a couple of Amish girls in the car that hit them—going over a hundred miles an hour. Can you imagine how terrible? What we know is that God's healing hand is wrapped around her and she plans to make her life here in the valley.

Which brings me to a second reason for this letter. Sara learned to be an EMT when she was living Englisch, and our bishop wondered if she might be called to be a Dokterfraa. I remember you telling me about Englisch Henry's Sarah and her becoming a Dokterfraa. Can you send me Sarah's address so that our Sara might write to her and learn what's involved in such a path? Thanks so much in advance.

We are all well here despite our surprises, and looking forward to Christmas, too. I was a little poorly in the autumn with a nausea I couldn't seem to shake, but it has tapered off now. I just get a stomach ache and terrible wind now and again. Reuben thinks I should make an appointment to see the Englisch doctor, but it's such a trip by bus down to Libby, especially in the winter. Maybe I'll think about it after Christmas, because there's for sure and certain no time before!

Take care, and our love to all.

Your cousin and sister in Christ,

Naomi Miller

NAOMI STAMPED the letter and stood it up between the salt and pepper shakers on the table for one of the boys to take down to the mailbox.

"I'll be so happy when little Joel comes to live here for good," she said to Sara, who had just finished feeding Nathan and was waiting for a satisfying burp. "He loves to go down to the mailbox, as though it's Christmas every time he opens it."

"I used to feel that way, too," Sara said with a smile. "One of the things about being Amish is that you can almost guarantee a letter from someone every day. I can't tell you how depressing it is to come home from a double shift and find nothing in the mailbox but ads for carpet cleaning."

"That *is* depressing," Malena said. "Especially if you don't have carpets." She was seated at the table with a piece of scratch paper, a pencil, and a fat eraser left over from their days as scholars, trying to make the lines of a new quilt design match what was in her head. Evidently she wasn't having much luck.

"To get a letter, you have to write one," her twin pointed out. "Isn't that right, you little darling?" She covered Nathan's face in kisses. "You're not taking him along today, are you?" she said to Sara, though the baby was in his sleeper, not in the freshly laundered snowsuit.

"Joshua wants to make a list of things that need to be repaired at the old place," Sara said. "It's not very baby friendly out there yet. So, *neh*. I hope Nathan won't be too much trouble once he gives me a burp." She patted his back and was rewarded by a healthy burp and a dribble of formula.

Naomi hadn't recovered from her first sentence. "Joshua? Going with you to the farm?"

As she wiped the baby's face, Sara said, "Apparently he and the bishop are cooking up a work frolic for the men, once they have the list."

"Isn't that *wunderbaar*," Naomi said faintly. *Well, forevermore,* Reuben's grandmother would have said, on hearing something this difficult to believe. Joshua had made a career out of avoiding the work at the ranch. His mind always seemed to be somewhere else, his hands doing anything else but what his father needed. And now he was preparing a list of jobs for a work frolic? Next they would hear he was actually volunteering to do some of them himself.

Something must have happened during his visit with Little Joe out there in the barn yesterday. She would probably never know what it had been, but if these were the results, she could only be grateful.

They heard Hester's hooves and the rattle of the buggy in the yard. "That's my cue," Sara said, and pulled on Malena's away bonnet over the knit cap on her head. She wore her *Englisch* puffy jacket, her feet warm in a new pair of wool socks. She kissed the baby good-bye and slipped out the door.

Naomi filled the kettle and put it on the stove to heat, then reached down a packet that Carrie had sent with her last letter. The *Dokterfraa* in Whinburg Township had said it was a nice mix that would settle her stomach. Naomi hoped it would help with heartburn, too. Honestly, it was difficult to grow old gracefully when your body was busy either embarrassing you or worrying you. This was not normal for her, not at all. She had the Glick constitution, which scoffed at things like heartburn.

If this went on until Christmas, maybe she would consider taking Reuben's suggestion more seriously. His *mammi*, whom he had adored, had died of stomach cancer, and she could see that memory in his worried eyes every time she was foolish enough to mention whatever was wrong that day.

First of all, she'd keep her complaints to herself. And then maybe she'd use that cell phone in the jar in the cupboard to make an appointment with the doctor.

It would be *gut* to know she was perfectly fine, and ease her husband's mind once and for all.

"So, what did Little Joe have to say to you last night?" Joshua drove the buggy out of the Circle M lane and turned right on to the county highway. It was the first chance they'd had to compare notes about the bishop's visit with no one around to overhear.

"A couple of *gut* things and a scary thing." Sara smoothed her green skirts over her legs, which were clad in warm black tights. Black snow boots completed her ensemble, thanks to the Amish variety store and the generosity of the Millers, who didn't seem to mind feeding her and clothing her, too.

"What were the good things?"

She told him—about being able to join church, about the possibility of learning to be a *Dokterfraa.* "And the scary thing is that I have to go before the *Gmee.* On my knees. To ask forgiveness."

He glanced at her, his hands tightening on the reins. "What for? What did you do that was so bad?"

She raised her eyebrows in a *duh* look, like an *Englisch* teenager. "I was in that car."

"Sara, that's not your fault. You could have been—"

"What? With *Mamm* and *Dat?* That guy still would have hit them. I just wouldn't be here right now to argue about it with you."

"You can't know that. One little change in that man's evening and he could have missed them. Taken a different road. Fallen down drunk and spent the night in the Sheriff's lockup. The point is, why do *you* have to ask forgiveness?"

For a hundred reasons. "Maybe I have to forgive myself."

"*Ja,* well, you don't have to go on your knees to the church to do that."

"Maybe I do. Maybe the church has to forgive me for being so wilful that it cost my family their lives."

He guided Hester into the first of three turns that would take them to the farm. "Do you really believe that? That you killed your family, and not the man at the wheel?"

The night exploded in her mind again. The crash into the buggy—the horses—the baby—

She gasped with a sob that came up out of nowhere. "I don't know," she wailed. "Yes! Yes, I do. I could have done something. Could have tried harder to stop him. Could have drunk less." She tried to catch her breath through her tears. "Anything to change just one second, so they could have got through that intersection!"

He swore and guided Hester over to the side of the road.

"Hey," he said. "Hey." He slid toward her and pulled her into a hug. "It's okay," he murmured while she shuddered and heaved. "It will be okay."

"It will never be okay," she cried into the wool of his coat. "Never."

Some truths you couldn't argue with, and he didn't try. He just held her until her weeping shivered into hiccups, and then into silence. When she moved to pull away, he silently lifted a hip and took a handkerchief out of his pocket.

"It's clean," he said.

She blew her nose and mopped her eyes while he flapped the reins over Hester's back and resumed their journey. "Sorry," she said hoarsely.

"For what? Having feelings? Having regrets? Seems to me you don't need to apologize for those. You're not alone."

"In having regrets? I suppose not." She took a breath. "Carey and Nathan?"

"Among other things, yeah."

They were on the last turn now. Soon they'd pass a poplar

windbreak and they'd be able to see the Fischer fields, all over-grown. Acres of dead weeds, frozen by winter.

"Never regret Nathan," she said suddenly. Fiercely. "My baby *Schweschder* is gone and I never even got to kiss her good-bye. She'll never say her first word, or go to school, or learn to cook with *Mamm*. But you..." Her throat closed up and she tried again. "You have that chance. To love him. Teach him. Be a family with him." The tears were coming again, the chest-shaking sobs. "Be grateful for every single moment, Joshua."

She buried her face in the hanky again, weeping so hard her ribs hurt. The hanky smelled like him, like cold sunshine and wood chips and horse. The smell, at this moment, of a kind of comfort.

Once more, he pulled Hester to a stop, only this time safely in the Fischer lane. "Come here," he said gruffly. Once more his arm went around her, pulled her against him. Once more she soaked the already damp front of his coat.

But this time, when the sobs died away, she didn't straighten and move to her own side. This time, she leaned against him. And he didn't seem inclined to pull away. "It's been a year since it was this bad," she said on a long, shud-dering sigh. "I wonder if it will ever get better."

"It has to," he said, his voice husky. "Otherwise, how could we survive the bad times?"

"We just do, I guess. We muddle through, with help. Like now."

"I'm not what you'd call much help."

She waggled the soaked hanky at him before she blew her nose on it.

"Okay, point taken. But I'm pretty much the biggest mess this valley has to offer."

"I'd argue that with you, since the biggest mess is sitting

right here." At last, she straightened and Joshua encouraged Hester to start down the lane. "What a pair."

"Messes we may be, and heading for a third mess, but at least the farm doesn't have to stay that way. I've got paper and a pencil for a list and we've got two hours before it starts to get dark."

At least he could make her smile.

He pulled up in front of the house, and tied Hester to the fence. "I brought some hay for her. I don't remember seeing a lot of forage last time."

With the horse looked after, they went around to the back, where once they were inside, Joshua made a note. "One. Replace glass in back door."

"Two," Sara said, eyeing the rat poop, the beer bottles, and the gouges in the kitchen table, "hire HazMat team to sterilize kitchen."

"*Ja*, no kidding. Is there a cellar? We'd better check it in case there's water damage."

She pointed him to the cellar door and he pulled a flashlight out of his coat pocket. "Careful," he said. "This could be where the rats came from."

"Oh, please don't tell me that," she groaned.

Still, she followed him down the steps. "Well, I guess I know where the other mattresses went." The place looked like a flophouse, and was freezing besides. "Why would they drag these down here? It's not like we have tornadoes. Okay. Three. Dispose of disgusting mattresses."

Mamm's pristine pantry was completely empty, except for broken canning jars and unidentified stains on the floor.

"Pickled beets?" she wondered aloud.

He shone the flashlight beam over her shoulder. "Blood? Four. Clean up pantry. At least there's no water damage."

When they went upstairs and climbed to the second floor, they found it needed a good clean, but was otherwise undamaged. The men didn't need to clean during their work frolic; she could do it herself.

"I can give you a hand," Joshua said. "Scrubbing walls and floors will go faster with two. Or maybe I can ask my sisters if they'll come along. Make a day of it."

"Fun for them," Sara said wryly.

"The thing about my sisters is they can make fun out of just about anything. Even beet blood on the pantry floor. Come on. We need to check the springhouse. Without running water, it'll be hard to clean anything."

The springhouse had been *Dat*'s pride and joy. The spring bubbled up out of the ground about a quarter of a mile up the hill. He had built the springhouse to protect it from weather and animals, and run pipes out of it. A little way down the slope the pipes entered a gravity-fed water storage tank of rigid plastic.

"How much?" Joshua asked. "Five thousand gallons? Three?"

"Your guess is as good as mine," Sara told him. "That's the springhouse, there."

It was just a shed, but built to last, the way *Dat* had done everything. Except …

"I see why you don't have any water pressure." Joshua put his hands on his hips. "I wonder when that happened?"

The roof had been torn clean off, probably during a nor'easter sweeping down from Canada. When they opened the door and went inside, there was no water visible in the spring—it was so clogged with decomposing leaves that it looked dry.

"Five," Sara said. "Get spring cleared and working again."

"Six," Joshua added. "Get mud and junk cleaned out of storage tank." He added them to his list. "I wonder how the pipes are?"

"First things first." Sara tried to clear away the leaves with the toe of her boot, and shook her head. "I need a hoe or a rake."

"*Dat* knows about springs and gravity feeds," Joshua told her. "If you're going to live here, you can come up with him and learn how to maintain it."

"Isn't that men's work?" she teased. "Aren't I supposed to be cleaning walls and floors?"

"It's all work. And my mother will be the first one to tell you that she checks the springhouse above our place every time she goes up to the orchard. One time she opened the door and an owl flew out. Scared her half to death, but she was glad she'd checked. Otherwise he'd probably have died in there."

Sara glanced into the corners of the springhouse, but there were no skeletons of any kind that she could see.

"Come on," she said. "We still have to check the barn."

That yielded several more entries on the list—repair the buggy, replace the rails and stalls, re-floor the loft, clean out the manure pit.

"The fences will need work," Joshua said, slipping the list into his pocket and gazing out over the broken fence at the fields. "But in early summer you might get a hay crop if the mulleins aren't too bad. That would bring in some cash. The Madisons are always looking for hay."

"The Madisons?"

"*Ja*, they're on the Rocking Diamond—the dude ranch up the road from us. I'm friends with the sons."

Was that who he'd been with on a Sunday morning,

drowning his sorrows in a tavern? "So the day we met, those were the friends you were with?"

He pushed off the fence and headed slowly in the direction of their buggy. "We'd all been on a bender the night before."

"Oh. Good friends, then."

He eyed her. "Don't you start."

"Oh, I won't. Been there, done that, never doing it again."

"You mean ... that night?"

"*Ja*. Cured me permanently. Even the smell of beer makes me a sick to my stomach."

"I guess it would." He sighed. "I get the feeling my drinking days are over, too, if I have to ..." His voice trailed away.

"Be a dad?" she said, on a guess.

"Yeah. That." He untied Hester, put the reins through their channel in the storm front, and climbed into the buggy.

At least he was thinking of it now, though whether being a dad included Seattle, she didn't have the courage to ask.

She climbed in the other door. "Look on the bright side. If you stop now, you won't get that burst-capillary look drinkers have. You know, the red cheeks and bloodshot eyes. You're a nice-looking man. Shame to spoil it."

He didn't answer, only clucked at Hester, who set off at a trot up the lane.

But in the fading light, Sara could see she'd made him blush. Which made her feel kind of funny inside. A warm kind of funny.

She'd never made a man blush before.

9

THAT EVENING, while Joshua fed Nathan in the sitting-room rocker, *Dat* looked over his list. Then he nodded thoughtfully.

"Some of these things won't take more than a few minutes. Like the mattresses. And some might take a couple of men a couple of hours."

"Like the springhouse," Joshua said. He switched Nathan carefully to the other arm, as *Mamm* had told him, and baby settled back to energetic sucking.

"*Ja*, the springhouse. Once the spring itself is cleared, the storage tank will have to be cleaned out. Filters replaced."

"Pipes, too, probably. They aren't exposed, though, so they might have survived those winters if people were using water."

"One *gut* thing about the squatters, I guess," his father said wryly.

His brother Adam came in and made himself comfortable on the sofa, at the other end from *Dat*. "Sara doesn't really plan to live there, does she?"

"I'm right here," she called from the kitchen, where she was helping the twins do the dishes. "And I don't know yet."

"The bishop thought that if it was made livable, Sara might be able to get a renter," Joshua said. Nathan finished the bottle, so he set it aside and pulled the baby up on his shoulder. He patted his back, scarcely bigger than his own paw. How fragile babies were. He was beginning to realize how lucky he was to have so much help in this department. *Mamm*'s instructions alone were worth the price of any number of baby books.

"That's a *gut* thought," his father said, having clearly looked at the bishop's suggestion from every angle. "By spring, folks will be hearing from relatives who want to come out and work on the ranches. There might be a young family needing a place."

"Or a couple of single men going in on the rent together," Rebecca suggested, coming to the big opening between kitchen and living room, dish towel in hand.

"*Ja,* though hired hands tend to stay in the bunkhouse on a ranch," Joshua pointed out.

"You could charge less rent if they made it up in labor," *Dat* said. "That way, you'd have a little income to pay the taxes, and improvements could be made by the renters over the summer."

"I like that." Sara joined Rebecca in the doorway. "Because I do want to pay those taxes. Not just this year's, but what I owe the church."

"All in good time," *Dat* said with a smile. "Calvin Bontrager isn't in such a hurry for it that he'll be banging on the door."

Calvin Bontrager was the deacon in charge of the church's funds. His daughter Susan had been hanging around the ranch in the autumn, hoping to catch Daniel's eye. But since Joshua's eldest brother had fallen for Lovina Lapp a second time—or maybe he'd never stopped—Susan had given up and they were spared her endlessly good-humored bossiness.

Nathan gave a series of burps and spit up on the towel on Joshua's shoulder. He wiped the baby's face, noticing as he did so that his cheeks seemed to be chubbier, and his grip on Joshua's finger seemed stronger than when he'd first come. Formula must agree with him.

Instead of getting up and putting him to bed, Joshua thought he might sit here for another few minutes. Going out to the barn didn't seem as appealing when there might be raisin pie after a while, and talking things over with *Dat* didn't happen so often. Usually Joshua lost his temper the minute his father began to speak, and stomped out. But *Dat* was in a thoughtful mood, going over possibilities for Sara.

Ja, any time they talked about Sara, Josh wanted to have a part in the conversation. He didn't feel proprietary about her. Not at all. More like he was looking out for her. She knew his deepest secret and he knew her deepest wound in a way his family didn't, unless she chose to tell them. She was the baby's nanny; he was the one who drove her where she needed to go. They were kind of in this together. So, if *Dat* and his brothers were going to make plans for her or the farm, he wanted to know about them.

"What do we think about the week after Christmas for a work frolic?" *Dat* asked Joshua, then glanced up at Sara to include her. "Maybe the Tuesday? I don't dare suggest next week, or every *Fraa* in the valley will be after me with a frying pan for taking their husbands away at such a busy family time."

"Your own *Fraa* included," *Mamm* said from the kitchen. "Zach, can you get me a pint of cream from the cold pantry, please?"

Zach went downstairs and returned a few minutes later with the cream. It could only mean whipped cream for pie. Joshua was full from dinner, but would never in a hundred years turn that down. "Poor baby," he said to the warm little bundle cradled against his chest. "No pie for you for months and months. You're missing out."

Dat chuckled. "I look forward to his first bite of his *Mammi*'s *gut* pie," he said. "What do you think, Joshua? Sara? Tuesday?"

"Sounds *wunderbaar* to me," Sara said.

Joshua nodded his agreement. "People will be looking for a work frolic after eating too much over Christmas."

From the kitchen came the sound of the hand beater as Zach was roped into whipping the cream.

Little Nathan's eyes closed, and his mouth worked as though he were anticipating raisin pie in his future. Joshua couldn't help the smile curving his lips at the whimsical thought. When he looked up, *Dat* was gazing at him with just the same kind of smile, which widened when he realized Josh had seen it.

"Ischt gut," he said simply. Then he went on, "I will get the word out among the families, then. Divide up men to collect supplies. Sara, do you have a preference for paint colors in the kitchen, once it is cleaned out?"

"You're going to paint, too?" she asked, her brows rising under her curly bangs. She was growing them out, since no Amish woman wore bangs.

"It needs it," Joshua pointed out. "Badly. In this district, we paint the house's exterior white or gray, but most folks around here do the insides in light colors."

"Except us," Adam said, waving a hand at the interior of the log house.

"Butter yellow with white trim, then," Sara said promptly. "And I can paint the rest of the house once we get the walls scrubbed down. The living room used to be pale green, but I think *Dat* must have got the paint on sale because it always reminded me of a hospital room. Maybe I'll change it to a really pale gray. Yellow and gray is nice together. Nothing too showy."

"I like it," Malena said to her sister. "I can see a white, yellow and gray quilt for the sofa, can't you?"

"As a housewarming gift," Rebecca said, nodding. "Once she has a sofa."

"If I rent the house, I'll stipulate that no harm is to come to it," Sara said with a smile. "Fastest way to lose the damage deposit is to mess with one of Malena's quilts."

Josh was almost sorry to have to take the baby out to change him and put him in his crib. It had been a long time since he'd been so included in his family's plans and laughter. Since he'd seen that look of warmth and approval in his father's eyes. It couldn't just be because he was pinned in his chair by the baby, could it? Doing the right thing by him, as *Mamm* had requested?

Maybe that was part of it. But not all. Maybe it was just that he usually headed out after supper, to walk over to the Rocking Diamond, or go out to the barn to read the guidebook about Seattle he kept hidden in an old saddle bag. He still could, he thought as he moseyed back in to the living room. But *Mamm* was dishing up the raisin pie, and only a crazy person would give *that* up.

Dear Bishop Wengerd,

I am happy to hear that things are going so well for you and Sadie out there in Rocky Mountain country. Your nephew Neil and his bride-to-be Anna Esch are making plans to return to Colorado for at least the first year or two of their marriage. He is well able to provide for her with his share in the buffalo ranch, and I understand her father will get his first glimpse of one of those creatures once they settle in. This is the result of reading too many Western novels! In any case, I believe they will include the Montana branch of the family in their wedding visits, so you can hear all about it when you see them.

You inquired about Amish folk acting as EMTs and what we do out here in Whinburg Township. I am happy to tell you that about sixty percent of the volunteer fire department are Amish, and there is even a young Mennonite woman among them who works just as hard as any man to do her duty well and support her community. The licensing is not a burden, either to the pocketbook or the spirit, so set your mind at rest about that. The crew tell me that there is no hardship in serving in this way.

While of course our people cannot drive the fire engine or the ambulance van, this is the only thing they cannot do. When a call comes in, a siren sounds, and the volunteers on every farm within earshot respond. The engine collects them on the way to the call.

There in Montana, where people are more spread out, I understand that these battery operated hand-held radios can act as the siren does here. The engine would pick up your young woman on the way to the call.

Gordonville responds to nearly a thousand calls a year, but in Whinburg, we may only have two or three hundred. It is a respectable and much needed service, and if your Englisch fire fighters will welcome an Amish person to assist with our folk, then I can see no reason why she should not be permitted to fill this place.

I hope we will see you out here sometime. My Evie sends her best greetings to Sadie. Our son Ben is living in California these days, and expecting a child with a woman to whom he is not married. But I still have hope that God's love will fill his heart and cause him to remember he has a family who care about him and dearly wish to see him again.

Your brother in Christ,

Bishop Daniel Troyer

IT WAS THE WEDNESDAY BEFORE CHRISTMAS, AND THE household was in an uproar of baking and cooking and cleaning while Sara looked after Nathan and tried to stay out of the way. With Christmas on Friday and church at the Yoder place two days later, there was a lot to do. Fortunately, the family were not expecting a houseful of visitors this year. As Rebecca said, laughing, "Unto us a child is given—I think that's enough for this year!"

Little Joe had walked over with the letter from Bishop Troyer, much to her surprise. Sara looked up from the spiky handwriting. "I didn't expect this," she said.

"Nor did I, I have to say," the bishop admitted.

"But just because there are Amish EMTs in Lancaster County, it doesn't follow that there should be any here." It wasn't her place to say what she wanted on this subject. If she was going to learn *Uffgeva* again, the giving up of one's own will, then this was what her old shift captain would call a "teaching moment."

"That is true," he said.

From his seat at the head of the table, Reuben gazed from one to the other and said not a word. He, too, would be guided by the bishop's decision on this matter. She was thankful that Reuben was the kind of man who kept his own counsel, only giving it when it was asked for. It was kind of nice, though, having him there for moral support. Joshua was out feeding the cattle with his brothers, and Reuben should have been out there, too, but he'd come in when he'd seen the tall figure striding up the lane, black fedora-style Montana hat pulled down over his ears.

Little Joe would only wear his church hat when calling in an official capacity, so Reuben had hurried in.

"However, I believe it is worth discussing among us," Little Joe went on. "I can see the benefit of having an Amish EMT to serve our folk. Not only for translation for the very young and the very old, but for everyday mishaps. Perhaps we would not call the *Englisch* ambulance for some small accident, but we might send for our own EMT first, to get an opinion of its severity."

Sara dared to nod, and tried not to hold Nathan too tightly in case he woke.

"That would be helpful," Reuben said quietly. "And this matter of the handheld radio?"

The bishop smiled. "We hardly need that when each family has a cell phone."

"You have a cell phone?" Sara said in surprise.

"*Ja,* many of the western churches have allowed it. We are spread out such long distances that sometimes safety depends on it," Little Joe said. "Especially during spring and fall, when we take the cattle up or down the mountains."

"I believe Naomi keeps it in a jar in the cupboard," Reuben said with a chuckle. "Like flour, or sugar."

"I still have mine," Sara said. "But I want to give it up. Sure, I could change the number and dedicate it only to calls for assistance, but that might lead to calls from the *Gmee,* and then calls to chat, and... You know how it goes."

Little Joe nodded. "If the fire department supplies them, I would not interfere. But there are other things to consider. These *Englisch* men at the station. And you, a woman alone. How would this look?"

"I didn't have any trouble in Portland, at my old station. We were a team. Everyone respected each other. And when we worked night shifts, we each had our own room." She smiled. "I was grateful many a time that *Mamm* taught me how to cook. No one on shift would dare do anything to offend me, in case I went to another shift and took my cooking with me."

Little Joe smiled, too. "I well remember Darla Fischer's chicken and dumplings. Like little clouds melting on the tongue."

"Bishop, we might pay a visit to the fire station," Reuben said. "Find out how they will arrange things with an Amish EMT, a woman. This solution of collecting her on the way to a call seems *gut* to me. We are right on the county road and they would have to pass us to reach this side of the valley."

"And if they require that I sleep at the station, like the others?" Sara asked.

"That would not look so *gut*," the bishop said, shaking his head. "I am afraid we would have to draw the line there. With men, it would not be such a difficulty. But with a woman? *Neh*. For your own sake, I could not allow it."

She bowed her head, taking in Nathan's little face, his mouth moving even in sleep. "*Ja*, as you say."

She was amazed that Amish EMTs even existed. The chance to take up a job she loved again, even with conditions, was like a gift from heaven. And if it turned out that the shift captains wouldn't make allowances for her, then so be it. She still had work to do here.

"I can keep up my license, can't I?" she asked. "If it's no burden, as Bishop Troyer says?"

"*Ja*, I see no reason why not," Little Joe told her, draining his cup. "At the very least, you can be a help to the *Gmee* with this license. Well, Reuben, shall we pay a call on the fire department?"

"I will get Hester harnessed." Reuben rose, collected his coat and hat, and went out to the barn.

When the two men departed, silence fell in the kitchen. Sara held the baby, rocking a little almost instinctively. How strange to have people go to bat for her. Was this what she had been missing all these years? She'd only ever seen the community as a prison, something to run away from as fast as possible. Now she saw it as a refuge.

And how, she wondered, did Joshua see it? "How can your daddy bear to think of leaving these people?" she whispered to the baby.

And why had it begun to matter to her what Joshua Miller did?

§

NAOMI CAME INTO THE KITCHEN TO FIND SARA MURMURING to the baby in her arms. The girl looked up. "Did you hear? I may be able to be an EMT again."

"*Ja*, I did. I'll be interested to hear the results of this visit to the fire station." She sat in the chair at the table Little Joe had occupied, wincing slightly.

"Are you all right, Naomi?"

"*Ja*, just a little backache. I'm pushing fifty, you know. These things happen."

"But you haven't been feeling all that well since I've been here. You really should go to the doctor."

"Why, when I have an EMT right here in my kitchen?" She held her arms out for the baby, and Sara got up and laid Nathan gently in them.

She fetched Naomi a cup of coffee, poured a dollop of cream in it just the way her hostess liked it, and resumed her own seat. "I'm an EMT, not a doctor. If you fell, I could put you on a backboard and immobilize you until the ambulance got here. But I've got no training in what goes on in a person's insides."

"Maybe I'll go after Christmas." Naomi had already decided to, she just hadn't told anyone. "After the work party. If I don't do something soon, Reuben will put me in the *Englisch* taxi himself and take me."

"Would you like me to make the appointment for you?"

"Would you do that? Her card is in the jar with the phone."

"In case of emergency, huh?" With a smile, Sara got up and called right away. After the appointment was made for Wednesday, she made one for a well-baby check with a pediatrician in the office during the same trip. "We're Amish," she explained to the girl on the other end. "We have to hire a van to come, so we want to get as much accomplished as we can."

When she hung up, Naomi said, "You're very efficient. I'd forgotten about inoculations and that kind of thing."

"He should certainly have a checkup. And it will be *gut* to go together. For moral support. That way, Reuben doesn't have to leave his work on the ranch. Or Joshua, for that matter."

Naomi's eyes were soft as she gazed down at her grandson. "More than twenty years ago, I held Joshua just like this. Nathan favors him, I think."

"Have you ever met the mother?"

Naomi shook her head. "It sounds as though Joshua barely met her himself." Her tone was dry. "I'm so disappointed in the pair of them. But now we have this little one, and it may be the making of that boy. Man, I suppose I should say." She looked up. "How old was your baby *Schweschder* when God took her to Himself? I've noticed how handy you are with Nathan."

Sara's face quivered before she took a deep breath and let it out. "Nine months. I remember her having to have her inoculations. Poor darling, she screamed all the way home. I was so thankful *Mamm* had called an *Englisch* taxi. It got us home before all three of us went deaf."

She was speaking more easily now. Almost surprised at being able to talk about her family with freedom. As though they were no longer a terrible secret she was forced to keep.

"Naomi, did you hear what the bishop said? About my having to ask the church for forgiveness?"

"*Neh*, but it does not surprise me. I have only seen the need for reconciliation once, before Little Joe was bishop, and it was a man who had been baptized and then left the fold. He had to come before us all on his knees, too. But he was willing. That is the key," she said softly. "Willingness makes the sacrifice of one's pride so much easier."

"I don't have a lot of pride left," Sara said, making circles on the table with her coffee mug. "But whatever it takes. He says baptism classes start on January twenty-fourth. I want to have it over with before then."

How wise this young woman was, Naomi thought. And how fearless in her humility.

Naomi gazed at the baby in her arms, sleeping with the kind of trust that cast out fear, too. Joshua's baby. Naomi's heart cracked with sorrow for her youngest son, so lost and so angry, for reasons none of them understood. Even Malena, to whom he was close, had no idea when it had all begun, or why ... only that the Amish way of life was like a trap to him. And like an animal caught in it, all he knew was his own fear and pain.

Help him, Lord, Naomi prayed silently. *Help my boy to love his son, and let Your perfect love cast out fear.*

10

REUBEN RETURNED JUST as the snow began to fall and his sons were in the barn putting up the two field horses after their labors. He drove the buggy in and jumped out to unharness Hester, so Joshua moved over to help on the other side.

"We're in for some snow tonight," Reuben said. "I can feel it in the air—that big silence before a heavy snowfall."

"Think people will be able to get to church on Sunday?" Joshua asked. It wouldn't be the first time the snow had been too deep for the horses to pull the buggies.

"Hard to say," his father said, his hands moving efficiently on the buckles while Joshua matched him on Hester's other side. "But I think we'll be glad it's only at Yoders' if we have to ski over."

"*Dat!*" His father's humor surprised a laugh out of Joshua. "*Mamm* will have something to say about that."

"I'd think so. But between her feeling poorly and that new baby of yours, I think if it gets too deep, we might be having church at home, or at least over at the bishop's."

"*Mamm* is feeling poorly?" She looked okay to Joshua—or

at least, no different than usual. Except for those spells when she couldn't hold down the odd meal. "That was just the flu, wasn't it?"

"*Ja*, I hope so," his father said. He carried the harness over to its rack while Joshua looked after Hester, giving her a good rubdown and some oats for good measure. "She seems to be doing better. I'm glad, because the Christmas service is her favorite out of the whole year."

It had been Joshua's favorite, too, as a boy. His sisters always used to tease him that he was the baby in the prophecy in Isaiah, because his birthday was December tenth and came the closest to Christmas of any of his siblings. At the Christmas concert in their one-room Amish school down the road, he'd played the part of the baby Jesus more than once just for that reason.

This year, he'd missed his birthday at home. The Madisons had rented a hotel suite in Whitefish and they'd taken him skiing to celebrate, and by the time he'd rolled into the Circle M, everyone had eaten his birthday cake. Which was fine. If they'd saved him a piece, it would already have been stale.

Barely two days later, he'd discovered he was a father. *Unto us a child is given.*

Or abandoned, as the case may be.

After freezing his feet off on the hay wagon for most of the day, walking into the house to the warmth of the woodstove felt like a blessing. The girls had been busy—not only had they been baking and cooking, they'd decorated the house for Christmas. On the kitchen table on a paper doily was the fat red, white, and green Christmas candle from the bookshop in Mountain Home. Two more waited to be lit Christmas morning on the side tables in the sitting room, and a wreath of pine hung on the front door, a bow of red ribbon setting off a trio of fat pine cones.

It was nothing like the Rocking Diamond, of course. Mrs Madison had arranged for delivery of a twelve-foot Christmas tree to stand in the big showpiece window of their living room, decorated by a professional who had come all the way from Missoula. This year's theme was music, so hanging from the branches were tiny gold and silver instruments. Horns, little pianos, musical notes, violins ... any instrument you could name became a decoration, forming a wonderland of gold and silver set off by fat lengths of red ribbon twisted among the branches, and about a million white twinkle lights. Instead of a star at the top, the decorator had placed a harp. Josh had heard that the *Englisch* sometimes put an angel up there, so he guessed that was as close as Mrs Madison was going to get.

But somehow, all that splendor didn't compare to walking into his own house and smelling the scent of pine combined with gingerbread and what had to be an elk roast. His stomach rambled and he realized that he'd been outside forking hay and getting lost in his own head, and had forgotten to come in to lunch.

After their silent grace, *Dat* carved the roast and everyone handed around their plates so that he could lay slices on each one. When he was done and the potatoes and vegetables began to make their rounds, *Dat* said to Sara, "We spoke to your friends at the volunteer fire department."

Sara looked up eagerly. "I've been trying not to ask, but I'm dying to know what they said."

"It turns out they were serious about a position for you, even without a driver's license. The captain read the letter that Bishop Troyer sent, and he seemed to agree that you could help out there in a modified capacity."

"Modified how?" Sara asked.

"They didn't like the idea of the siren. Neither do I. Scares the cattle." *Dat* shoveled a bite of meat and potatoes into his mouth. "But the hand-held radio might a possibility. They use those already. And there would be no working on Sundays."

"Of course not," *Mamm* said.

"What about shift work?" Sara looked uneasy. Joshua wished she'd eat. She was too skinny to start with, and the elk roast was *wunderbaar*.

"The captain said that when they needed you, it would be on a call-by-call basis," *Dat* reported. Sara nodded, and finally picked up her fork. "You wouldn't stay overnight. It isn't suitable. Even he agreed about that. But some day shifts, especially weekends." He twinkled at her. "They want to sample your cooking."

Sara smiled and ate a few bites, but it didn't seem to Josh that she tasted a single thing. "I can hardly believe it. A job, just like that. Even if it is on-call only, at least I can get more experience, and help on calls to the *Gmee*."

"He says that if you really meant it, you should go over and fill out some paperwork," *Dat* went on. "But I ask you, before we get too hasty, have you talked this over with Naomi and Joshua?"

"Me?" Joshua blurted. "What have I got to do with it?"

"Did you forget so soon that she's supposed to be Nathan's nanny?" Malena demanded. "How did this all come about, Sara? How are you going to manage two jobs?"

"I'm not quite sure," Sara said. "I stopped in to ask them about a job before I knew you folks were serious about earning my keep as a nanny. I was desperate to find a way to bring in some money. I guess I should have thought it through before so many people went to such trouble to make it possible."

"There is still time to think about it," *Dat* said. "The captain said he would be making no changes until the new year." He paused. "He wishes us a merry Christmas. I wished him the same."

"I wouldn't mind being a volunteer fireman myself," Zach said unexpectedly.

Mamm put down her knife and fork to stare at him.

"It would be *gut* to have those skills," he said. "To be an EMT like Sara. I was talking with Dave Yoder about it, and he's interested, too. We just never thought it was possible, since we don't drive cars."

"It seems it is possible," Adam said, looking from his brother to Sara. "If the bishop and *Dat* agree that Sara can do it, maybe you and Dave can, too. They can probably use all the hands they can get."

"Let's not let that horse run away with you," *Mamm* told Zach. "David's father will need to talk it over with the bishop."

"Oh, *ja*, I know," Zach said cheerfully. "But it would be *gut* to help out. And get paid a wage for it. Besides, someone has to look out for Sara."

She smiled at him. "I'll be the one looking out for you. Helping you study for the license exam, being the dummy you practice CPR on, that kind of thing."

"They're on that runaway horse," *Mamm* said helplessly to *Dat*. "Or like a bunch of cattle all going down the wrong trail."

But Joshua could tell she didn't really mean it. Her eyes were twinkling and she had said no to what Zach wanted maybe twice in living memory. He turned his attention to his roasted squash. If anyone should join the volunteer fire department, it should be him. He was the man with the driver's license, even if *Mamm* and Sara seemed to have forgotten about it.

Which was just as well. The last thing he wanted to do was bring *that* to his father's recollection.

A cry came from down the hall and he gulped the last of his vegetables. Nathan was awake. He pushed out his chair to go and take care of the baby. Sara got up too. As he walked back to the bedroom, he heard her open the door of the refrigerator. Water ran into a pot. When he'd cleaned and changed the baby and brought him out to the kitchen, she was just testing the liquid on her wrist.

"Ready," she said with a smile.

His mother settled back to finish her supper in a leisurely fashion. He refused to look at her, but he would bet anything she was exchanging a glance with *Dat*.

Fine. Sara was the baby's nanny. Of course she would get up from the table to help him see to Nathan's needs. There was no reason to think any more of it.

He was still going to Seattle, no matter what. He just had to figure out a way to do it now that his life had become so complicated.

THE AMISH OF THE SIKSIKA VALLEY, LIKE MANY OTHER communities, kept both first and second Christmas, or, as *Daadi* Miller used to call it when he was alive, Old Christmas. The first was December 25, and was a joyful time of family carols, friends visiting, and a big meal. Old Christmas was twelve days later, on January 6. Sara's family had celebrated it with more solemnity, even fasting before the big family meal, and spending the day quietly in board games and reading.

What a difference there was between last year's Christmas in Portland and this year! For an EMT, Christmas was busy, and the calls came in relentlessly through all three shifts. For many, Christmas was not the happy family season it was cracked up to be, and the fire crew fielded calls from medical emergencies to rescues of all kinds. Even rescuing people from themselves. Christmas could be hard on those without family or any kind of support, and Sara had spent more than one long night thankful that she had work to do and a team to do it with, or she might have been one of those people. "There but for the grace of God go I," she'd thought many a time, seeing the damage that loneliness and isolation could do.

And now here she was on the Circle M, which she would never have predicted a year ago, in the middle of the happy chaos that was the Miller family.

It was Christmas Eve, and Rebecca had just lit the Christmas candles. While the Coleman pole lamp illuminated the kitchen as usual, the softer light of glass kerosene lamps glowed in the sitting room. The fire in the woodstove was so cozy that you could almost forget it was snowing outside if you couldn't hear the whisper of snowflakes against the windows. With Nathan clean and dry in her arms, Sara settled on the sofa next to Naomi and Malena. The boys ranged themselves around the room while Reuben opened the big family Bible on his lap and put his glasses on his nose.

She slid a look at Joshua, and felt a tingle of shock when she realized he had been watching her. He got up and came over to sit in the ladderback chair next to her corner of the sofa. "Want me to take him?"

Without a word, she transferred the warm bundle into his arms. Nathan blinked up at his father and his rosebud lips stretched.

"He smiled at me." Joshua's voice held surprise and a tinge of pleasure.

"Likely it was gas," Naomi said.

But Joshua shook his head. "It was a smile. I know it. Wasn't it, little *Gefunnenes*?"

"Hey, he's not a foundling," Sara protested, leaning over the arm of the sofa to look into the baby's face. "Are you, pumpkin? You have a family and *ein Vater* right here."

"He's not a pumpkin, either, if you're splitting hairs," Joshua said. "And it was too a smile. Look, he's smiling again."

Clearly gas, but Sara wasn't about to burst his bubble. "Merry Christmas to us, then," she said. "A baby's smile is better than any Christmas present."

Reuben cleared his throat, and Sara settled back into the sofa. *"There was in the days of Herod the king of Judaea, a certain priest named Zacharias, of the course of Abia: and his wife was of the daughters of Aaron, and her name was Elisabeth ..."*

Sara hadn't heard the Christmas story from the book of Luke since her father had read it, the winter before the accident. Somehow it just wasn't the same read by a stranger over the radio while you sat in Portland's rush-hour traffic. And since she hadn't gone to church or cracked a Bible when she was living *Englisch*, she'd never heard it there, either. So really, tonight it was like hearing it for the first time, seeing it play out in her imagination.

"And the angel said unto them, Fear not: for, behold, I bring you good tidings of great joy, which shall be to all people..."

Nathan murmured, and Joshua spoke to him softly, the baby's head cradled against his chest.

Sara glanced around the room to see that all the women—Naomi, herself, Malena, and Rebecca—were watching them. Naomi's face was soft with love, and Sara thought there might be tears welling in her eyes. The twins were gazing at their brother as though he were a puzzle they were trying to figure out. Sara was certain that she was the only person in the room who knew about his plan to jump the fence and go to Seattle, which might have solved the puzzle of their brother for them. But it wasn't her place to reveal his secret.

She wasn't entirely sure what her place was going to be. For a person who had arrived with eighty dollars in her pocket and zero prospects, she now had a farm and more than one path to choose from.

"And the child grew, and waxed strong in spirit, filled with wisdom: and the grace of God was upon him." Reuben closed the big Bible reverently.

And at that moment, Adam, the third Miller son, launched into "Angels We Have Heard on High," and the family joined in, singing from memory. Sara hadn't realized that he had such a nice voice. After that, they sang "Joy to the World" and "O Little Town of Bethlehem" and a couple of others that Sara hadn't heard since she'd been a child, learning them for the Christmas concert in the schoolhouse. She wasn't much of a singer, but at least she knew the tunes and enough of the words that she could hold up her end. Even Joshua sang, though it was more of a lullaby, as though he thought he might frighten the baby if he sang too loudly, or took deep breaths.

Afterward, Naomi and the girls served up the sour cream cherry pie Rebecca had made that afternoon.

"What are your plans for tomorrow?" Reuben asked, licking his fork with relish. "Your mother and I will stay home after our meal, in case we have visitors."

Christmas visits, Sara remembered, were another tradition she'd forgotten in the *Englisch* world.

"Depends on the snow, I guess," Zach said. "But me and Adam were thinking of going over to Yoders'. We can always go on skis if it's too deep for the buggy."

"I'm staying home, too," Rebecca said. "Sara, if you wanted to do some visiting, I can look after Nathan."

"Oh." She probably sounded as surprised as she felt. "I hadn't really—I mean, it's been so long that—"

"She'll see everyone in church Sunday," Malena told her twin. "People come and go, don't they. Some she knew growing up may have moved away."

"If she drove out to the Bontragers' old place, she'd find the Eichers living there now," Zach said with a laugh. "But if you want to come over to Yoders' with us, Sara, you'd be welcome. Dave and Phil have two sisters at home yet. The oldest one got married last year."

The oldest one. Dinah Yoder. She'd been in the car with her that night. "Honestly," she said, "I'd just as soon stay home."

"It's not because of … what the bishop said?" Reuben asked, as though he hesitated to poke his nose into her business.

"About the reconciliation?" Sara shook her head. "At least— Well, all right, maybe I do feel a little shy about seeing people. Wondering what they think. Once I'm reconciled, it will be different. Behind me. Done and over with."

Had Dinah also had to go through it? Had she told anyone about that night?

"You're so brave," Rebecca said. "I don't know if I would have the courage to face the whole *Gmee*." She got up to collect the empty plates and forks.

"It's not like she has a choice," Joshua pointed out.

"Oh, I think I do," Sara said before Reuben could straighten up and remonstrate with his son. If Joshua tensed up to defend himself, Nathan would be frightened. "The bishop hinted that I could wait until I was baptized, when the past would be all washed away anyhow. But I told him I wanted to do it before I began baptism classes. It just seems ... right. In the right order, you know?"

"That's very wise," Naomi said. "You must do as the Spirit prompts you. And whatever happens, you will have us with you, so you don't need to feel embarrassed or afraid."

"I don't know what I would do without you," Sara said quietly, her own gaze soft on Naomi. "Or where I'd be. Freezing in an empty house and burning the kitchen table for firewood, probably."

"The *Gmee* would not have allowed that," Reuben assured her. "But all the same, I will be glad when we've given the place a once-over in our work frolic on Tuesday." He leaned forward, his hands clasped. "We will pray, and then I will say *guder nacht*. Tomorrow will be a busy day."

They bowed their heads in unison and said the Lord's prayer together.

Even Joshua.

11

THOUGH SHE SHOULD'VE BEEN tired after a busy day of baking and baby care, Sara didn't feel sleepy enough to climb the stairs and go to bed with the other girls. Reuben and Naomi were probably asleep by now, and Adam and Zach had gone up a few minutes ago, but Joshua still sat in his hard chair, holding Nathan. Did he plan to sleep there?

"There are probably more comfortable chairs in here," she suggested from her comfortable corner of the sofa. She tucked her sock feet up under her skirts, pulled over a crocheted cushion, and made herself even more comfortable against the arm.

"I don't want to move in case I disturb him and he won't go down."

"Not likely. That kid is out until midnight snack time."

"When do they start sleeping through the night?" Joshua wanted to know in a low voice.

"You'd have to ask your mother. But I think five or six months?" Sara tried to remember. "I suppose every baby is different."

"He seems like a pretty happy guy so far, though."

"He does." She reached over and gave him a nudge. "He'll be fine. Come over and share the sofa if you're not going to bed."

At last he got up and, the baby nestled in one arm, settled gingerly on the other end of the sofa. He could reach out and tickle her knee, or she could slide her feet under his leg to keep them warm. Neither of which was appropriate, and would probably make him leap up and run for the hills. Or at least the Rocking Diamond.

Speaking of ... "No big Christmas plans with the Madisons?"

He gave a one-shoulder shrug so as not to disturb Nathan. "Haven't decided yet. They have open house for all their business contacts later in the afternoon. The spread they put on is almost as famous in the valley as *Mamm*'s elk stew. But..." His voice trailed off.

"But?"

He glanced at her. "I don't know. Maybe I would go ... if I had a date."

Her eyebrows rose. "This is news. Are you seeing someone? Does she know about Nathan?"

"No, silly. I meant you. We could go together. Trust me, the food is worth being seen in public with the likes of me."

"You are perfectly presentable in public," she said, "as long as you take a shower first and ease up on the beer. Are you one of the Madisons' business contacts?"

He gave a half smile, and shook his head. "Technically, *Dat* is. He leases one of their allotments because they don't use it for grazing cattle. They take guests up there for trail rides, but that's not really what the allotments are for. Our cattle add to the experience, apparently."

"So you'd be representing the family," Sara suggested. "Nothing wrong with that. As long as the other guests don't object to Amish folks among their august company."

"I heard that Little Joe went once, but not a second time." Joshua grinned outright. Again Sara was struck by the way it changed his face. He had a pair of deep dimples in his cheeks that probably made all the girls in Talley's swoon. "It takes a lot to scare Little Joe Wengerd, but I think Mrs Madison did him in."

"Does she scare you?"

He shook his head. "I don't see much of her. I'm usually out with the boys."

"Ah, the infamous Madison boys." She nodded wisely. "Maybe it would be worth the price of admission to meet them. Then I would know who to avoid in town."

Again that grin, and she tried not to stare at the dimples. "I'd put you up against all three of them together, believe me. Any girl who's a volunteer fire fighter and hauling those hoses around probably has muscles they don't want to tangle with."

"An Amish girl wouldn't dream of tangling with them," she said with mock primness. "But what if you do? Are you going to ditch me to take off with them? Make me hitch a ride home with somebody?"

He glanced at her, surprised. "You think I would do that?"

"I don't know. You're the guy I found drinking in a bar after a bender with those guys, remember?"

"Yeah, but things are different now."

Were they really? He'd just invited her to go with him to a worldly family's home on Christmas Day, a day when his own family would be welcoming visitors. Was it because he felt ashamed to see people from the church? Or was it simply that he was looking forward to Mrs Madison's famous spread?

"Do many from the *Gmee* come to this shindig?" she finally asked.

"One or two, mostly the men, and never for very long. I mean, the *Englisch* around here are so used to doing all kinds of business with us that it never occurs to them there's much difference, except for the buggies. We might not wear a Stetson or a Resistol, but our work boots are the same, and we take our horses to the same farrier to be shod, and we shop at all the same stores in Mountain Home. It's mostly the big ranchers from other places who look at us sideways and try to make awkward conversation."

"*Us. We.* You're using those words as though you plan to stick around."

All the humor leached out of his gaze. "Keep your voice down."

Obligingly, she dropped her volume almost to a whisper. "Do you?"

He frowned at the baby on his arm, who was sound asleep. The whispering, Sara knew, wasn't for his benefit, but for anyone still awake upstairs.

"Nothing's changed."

"You still plan to go? Even with Nathan?"

"I haven't figured out that part yet. I might have to find work off the ranch in the new year. Or worst case, wait until next year's share of the cattle money."

"That comes in the autumn?"

He nodded. "Nathan will be older, and not so frail, maybe."

"Ten or eleven months is still pretty young to travel with a baby. And you might not find anyone to look after him right away."

"*Ja,* for sure and certain I know that!" His whisper was a hiss of irritation.

"Would it be so bad to stay?" she asked after a moment, a wistful note in her almost-whisper.

"And join church?" He shook his head. "If I stay, I'll have to do that, and I don't think I can."

"I thought that, once," she said on a sigh. "And *der Herr* put roadblocks in all the roads except the one that led here. It took a long time to accept that coming back was the best thing to do. The only thing, really."

"How do you figure that?" he asked. "He blocked you being an EMT?"

"Not so much that, but when it came time for promotion, I was the best candidate and didn't get it. My friend the dispatcher said it was because I'm a woman, but I don't believe it. Our captain was a fair man. Someone else said it was because one of the brass had a brother-in-law who needed the job. I figure that was more likely. In any case, I'm not completely clueless. Along with a few other things that happened, I finally realized *der Herr* was managing a cosmic conspiracy to get me back here." She chuckled, more a couple of puffs of air than anything. But at least she could see the humor in the situation.

She wasn't so sure Joshua could.

After a few minutes of sitting in silence, where it seemed he was thinking over what she'd said—or maybe he was contemplating the Christmas party at the Rocking Diamond— she swung her legs off the sofa and stood.

"I'm going to bed. Want me to put Nathan in his crib?"

"No, I'll do it. Sure you won't go with me?"

"What, to your bedroom?" Her eyebrows rose under her bangs, and she felt a tingle of the forbidden that she squelched immediately.

He rolled his eyes. "No. To the Rocking Diamond. Tomorrow."

Oh. "Why not. It might be fun. And I'd get to meet the scary Mrs Madison. Beard her in her beautifully decorated den."

"Famous last words," he said, shaking his head as he got up.

At least he was smiling again. And for that, maybe it was worth giving up her first Christmas at the Circle M to mingle with a bunch of worldly strangers, all dressed to the teeth.

❧

SINCE HE WAS REPRESENTING THE CIRCLE M, JOSHUA dressed Amish to go to the party. He even told *Dat* where he and Sara were going, and for what purpose.

"Sara is willing for this?" Reuben said in disbelief, his gaze moving from Joshua to her. "I thought you were staying home."

"Joshua invited me. I thought it would be a good opportunity to meet our *Englisch* neighbors, since I'm meeting the Amish ones tomorrow at church." Sara paused. "It will be the most people in one place that I've seen since Portland. Scary thought."

"You will be fine," Naomi said, coming to the door to see them off. "We'll take good care of Nathan. And be sure to give our greetings to Brock and Taylor Madison."

Since the snow was two feet deep, with more threatened later tonight, Joshua had dug out the two-seater sleigh that morning and cleared the hay and chicken deposits out of it. "Jupiter is our field horse," he explained as he shook the reins over his back. "He's as strong as an ox and a couple of hands higher than Hester. Good for snow."

He hadn't meant it to, but the one-horse open sleigh pulling up in the Rocking Diamond's circular sweep caused a sensation. "Oh, look at that!" a lady in a fake fur coat trilled, whipping out her phone to snap pictures.

"They're Amish, Meredith," her husband said, tugging on her sleeve. "They don't like their pictures taken."

Too late. Cameras clicked from up on the vast deck, from the living room windows, even from cars pulling up behind them. They'd be on Facebook within the hour. But since neither he nor Sara had joined church, it was all probably moot, and would give the *Youngie* a laugh when they saw the images.

He unhitched Jupiter so he didn't have to stand in the cold for however long he and Sara lasted inside, and took him into the barn.

Barn, ha. You could house six Amish families in here quite happily. It sparkled with cleanliness and each of the horses looked to be well taken care of. Not that their own weren't. But the Circle M cutting horses had a healthy lack of fat that told the world they were working animals. The most work some of these animals saw was a seven-day trek up to the grazing allotments, and a daily gallop in the field when Mrs Madison took them out for exercise.

In the house, someone dressed in black slacks and a white Western shirt with a bolo tie relieved them of their coats and coverings. The boy hesitated, glancing at Sara's pristine white *Kapp*. "I keep this one on," she assured him with a smile.

Sara took in the house with its huge staircase to the upper floor, where a balcony ran from one end to the other and gave access to the family's rooms. The living room had to be fifteen hundred square feet all by itself, with massive floor-to-ceiling windows, a river rock fireplace two stories high, and leather sofas with wool Pendleton blankets thrown carelessly over their backs.

"How rich are these people?" Sara murmured to him as they made their way toward the Madisons, who were receiving in front of the Christmas tree. "I didn't think dude ranches paid this well."

"Ten thousand a week, per couple, to stay in the guest cabins here," he murmured.

She made a sound and covered her mouth.

"They breed and train horses, too," he went on quietly as they approached their hosts. "Out there in the barn is a horse belonging to a Saudi prince."

"I take it back," she said, looking as though she was about to burst into hysterical laughter. "What are we doing here again?"

But the Madisons had spotted them—not difficult, since Amish folks were few and far between in this crowd. "Joshua," Brock Madison boomed. "Haven't seen you in a few days. How are you?"

"I'm well, thanks," he said, shaking the man's hand. "Merry Christmas."

"And to you," Taylor Madison said, leaning in to kiss him on the cheek. Her blond bob gleamed gold in all the twinkle lights adorning the tree. "I see you've brought a friend."

"This is Sara Fischer," he said as she shook hands with the couple. "She used to live here, and now she's back. She's staying with us."

"It's nice to meet you, Sara," Mrs Madison said, taking in Sara's tall, slender form. "Fischer. Why is that name ringing a bell? Do we know your family?"

"I don't think so," Sara said. "They were killed a little over five years ago. Car accident."

"Oh, I'm so sorry." Mrs Madison's perfectly manicured fingers touched her lips, as though to bring the words back, and her blue eyes widened. "That's why I remembered. I read about it in the paper. How awful. You poor girl. Are the Millers taking good care of you?"

"Yes, ma'am," Sara said. "They're a wonderful family."

"We know," Mr Madison said, as though he'd had a hand in it. "I count Reuben Miller among my friends. Is he coming, Josh?"

"No, I'm representing the family today," he said easily. "Mom and Dad are expecting a stream of company this afternoon. They send their best greetings."

"You know the Fischers, Brock," Mrs Madison said, tapping his arm. "They owned that hay farm I wanted to buy. Out on Dutchman Road, remember?"

"Sure," her husband said. "But Taylor, maybe now is not the—"

"I heard a rumor it was going to be sold for back taxes, but it got snaked out from under me." She looked as though she were trying to frown, but she'd had some kind of operation that prevented it. "Who owns it now?" she said to Sara.

"I suppose I do, ma'am." Sara's cheeks had lost their color. "I'm going to be living there."

"Are you?" Mrs Taylor said in surprise. "Well, if you ever want to sell, I'll give you a darned good price. Half a million seem reasonable?"

Sara's mouth fell open. "I'm ... not planning to sell."

Mr Madison laughed. "Some Christmas present that would be! 'Tis the season," he said, slapping Josh on the back so that he almost staggered. "Help yourself to a plate of food and whatever you want to drink, and enjoy yourselves."

Josh took this as a signal to move along. "Thank you for having us."

"You'll probably find the boys over at the bar," Mrs Madison said by way of farewell as she turned to greet her next group of guests.

"The boys?" Sara repeated, as though she'd barely heard her, but following Joshua over to the long buffet tables. They were loaded with so much food it was surprising they didn't bend in the middle.

"Trey, Chance, and Clint. There, behind the punch bowl."

"Is she for real?"

"Who? Mrs Madison?" He paused in heaping his plate with everything from sausage rolls to little cheese packages in flaky pastry to broiled asparagus and smoked salmon.

"*Ja*, that woman who just offered me half a million dollars. She can't mean it. Was that her idea of a joke?"

"I doubt it. She probably does mean it. And so do you. You're going to live there, right?"

"Right." She seemed to gather her wits. "Of course I am. Are you going to eat all that, after the Christmas dinner you just put away?"

"*Ja*. Try these cheese things. They're really good." And when she opened her mouth to speak, he popped one in.

"Mmph!" Then, "Wow, they really are. Camembert. Hand me a plate, will you?"

What was the matter with him? Had he really fed her a cheese pastry in full view of everyone? Or was it because Chance was looking their way and he wanted to show him Sara was off-limits?

Which she wasn't. She could handle Chance if he decided he needed someone to play with.

She had held her own during Mrs Madison's inquisition, which would have made anyone else dissolve into tears. Taylor Madison had absolutely no filters. She said whatever she wanted, regardless of anybody's feelings. Regardless of whether someone had lost their family and was one step away from being homeless. Her money and beauty shielded her from offense, and most people put up with it because the couple were valuable friends to have in the valley, if you were *Englisch*. And sometimes even Amish.

"Hey, Miller." Chance and his brothers ambled over. "Merry merry and all that."

"Hey, Chance." He introduced Sara.

Trey, the eldest at twenty-four, tilted his head and gave her the once-over. "I didn't think you looked like one of Josh's sisters. Something about you doesn't say Amish, though. Maybe the Tony Lamas."

She shrugged. "Something about you doesn't say polite. Maybe the snotty attitude."

"Whoa." He pretended to stagger back, while his brothers got in a laugh at his expense. "My mistake, little lady. Let's start over. I'm Trey Madison." He offered his hand.

She took it and gave him a smile so warm he blinked. "Nice to meet you, Trey. Pretty place you have here."

"That's more like it." He didn't release her hand. Instead, Josh could swear he squeezed it just a little more.

Oh-oh.

Sara fluttered her lashes at him and squeezed back. Then applied just a little more pressure. Trey's face reddened, but he didn't let go.

Sara pulled him closer, and since they were the same height, leaned over to whisper in his ear while his knees sagged at the pain in his hand. "Wanna arm wrestle later?" she crooned.

"No," he said, the word coming out in a squeak.

"Aw, shame." She released him and stepped back, pouting. "It would've been fun."

Trey, the spoiled older son, suddenly found someone more interesting on the other side of the big room, and sauntered away without another word. Clint, the youngest, tipped back his beer.

Chance looked as though he was trying not to laugh. "It's really nice to meet you, Sara," he finally managed. "I could have sold tickets to that."

"She's an EMT," Joshua said. "It's the hoses."

"An Amish EMT? Seriously?" Chance's gaze was definitely interested now. "Like, in an ambulance?"

She nodded. "I'd like to get on at the volunteer fire department here. But we'll see. It's kind of complicated without a driver's license."

"Somehow I don't think complicated is going to bother you," Chance said. "Can I get you a drink?"

"Soda water and lime, if you have it."

"If we have it," Clint scoffed, and walked off to get it for her before Chance could move. Nobody was asking Josh if he wanted anything to drink, he noticed.

"Josh tells me you have a Saudi prince's horse out there in the barn," Sara said around a cheese pastry. "Truly?"

Chance nodded. "He's the most beautiful horse I've ever seen, and I've been around them all my life. He's Mom's pet project. No one but her is allowed to train him. Do you want to see him?"

Sara glanced at Josh. "Maybe another time. How long is he here for?"

"End of next summer, I think. The prince wants to enter him in some big horse show before he breeds him. But that's

Mom's department, not mine. I just make sure his stall is spotless in case a big black helicopter lands in our field unexpectedly."

"Does that happen a lot?" Sara looked amused.

"Twice since we got him in the spring. The guy is nuts about his horse. He's talking about buying a spread over east somewhere so he can have him on his own place, with his own staff. But whatever." Chance shrugged. "It's business."

"What about that movie star you were talking about?" Josh said. "Is he still coming?"

"Supposed to be. In the summer."

"What movie star?" Sara asked.

"I thought you Amish didn't have TV or go to movies."

"I lived on the coast for a number of years," Sara said. "Lived *Englisch*. I can read a *People* magazine the right way up."

He laughed. "I guess you can. His name is Quinn North. Heard of him?"

"That guy who did that space station series on Netflix, right?"

Josh stared at her. She sounded so worldly. This was the girl who was going to start baptism classes next month? Who sang *"Wo ist Jesus, Mein Verlangen"* slightly off-key while she bathed his son?

"That's him. It's all in negotiations, but apparently he's signed up to do a cowboy movie. Supposed to come here to learn how to rope and ride."

"You do that here?" she wanted to know. "Along with trail rides and such?"

"I guess we will, if he comes." Chance tilted his chin at Josh. "Though this guy should be the one teaching him. He's way better at it than any of us."

"If you spent more time with cattle and less with booze,

you'd be good, too," Josh said.

Clint rejoined them and handed Sara a tall glass that clinked with ice and had a lime wedge floating in it. "Sorry it took so long. A bunch of girls got there ahead of me."

"Thanks." Sara took a sip, then frowned. Took another. "Clint?"

"Yeah? Did I get it wrong? Did you want lemon?"

"This isn't soda water. It's vodka and tonic." She handed it back to him.

"You know what vodka tastes like?" His cheeks reddened.

Joshua suddenly noticed that Trey was back at the bar, surrounded by the girls, but watching them. "That was a dirty trick," he said, frowning. "Did Trey put you up to it?"

"Trey? No. I must've got the wrong glass. Let me go get another one." He was talking too fast, and made his escape.

Sara shook her head. "Nothing like putting your little brother up to your own dirty work. What was the point? To see an Amish girl drunk and dancing on the table?"

"I apologize for both of them," Chance said. "They're not like that normally, honest."

"I'm sure they're perfect gentlemen," she said with another smile that Josh now recognized as completely fake. "Josh, if you've seen everyone you'd like to speak to, I'd like to go home."

"Go home?" Chance repeated. "You just got here. Besides, Miller's always the last man standing."

If they stayed longer, Trey would probably get even more liquored up and demand that arm-wrestling match. Chance would ply Josh with beer until he couldn't see straight. And once again he'd be passed out in the bunkhouse with no memory of a good time to make the hangover worthwhile.

Sara shoulders straightened. "All right." Then, to Josh, "If you help me hitch up Jupiter I'll drive him home."

"C'mon, Sara, stay," Chance pleaded. "There's an afterparty out in the bunkhouse for a few of our personal friends. It'll be a great time."

Joshua made up his mind. She'd never driven Jupiter before and for all he knew, had never driven a sleigh, either. "I'm ready." He gulped the rest of the food on his plate and it vanished into the hands of another young man dressed in black and white. Sara's followed in another moment.

He left Chance Madison gazing after them with a perplexed expression, as though he'd never known Josh to be capable of saying no.

Well, you learned something new every day, *nix?*

They'd made it halfway to the big staircase and the coat room beneath it when someone called his name. He turned to see John Cooper, hand outstretched, dressed to the nines in a tobacco tweed Western jacket and a bolo tie of finely braided leather he'd probably made himself.

"Joshua," he said, his brown eyes warm with pleasure. "I was hoping to see you here."

Cooper was one of the kindest and most skilled men Joshua knew. "John," he said, grasping his hand. Then he stepped back. "Sara Fischer, this is John Cooper. He's one of the best known saddle and tack makers in the country. He has a workshop over by Siksika Lake." As she shook hands, Josh went on, "Is your wife with you?"

Cooper shook his head. To Sara, he said, "Kiara is a watercolor painter. She's half Kootenai, and specializes in the connection between tribal belief and art. She's got a show coming up, so time is short." He lowered his voice. "And truth be told, she's not a huge fan of Taylor Madison."

"She's not alone," Sara replied in the same confidential

tone, and gave him a smile that was definitely not the fake one.

Josh glanced at Sara, hoping his next question wouldn't overstep a boundary they'd never established. At the same time, opportunities like this didn't often drop into his lap. "John, I wanted to ask you ... Sara's father was a harness maker. He died some years ago, leaving a nice collection of tools. I wonder if you knew of anyone who might be able to value them?"

Sara raised an eyebrow at him.

"Just so you'd know," he said to her hastily. "In case someone in the *Gmee* made you an offer, you'd know if it was fair, right?"

"Do we have a harness maker in the district?" she asked after a pause.

"Just me," Cooper said modestly. "And I don't work on the Amish equipment. Men who specialize in that are few and far between. If your cutting horse needed a new saddle, I could help. But a buggy rig?" He shook his head. "Joshua probably knows more about that than I do."

"But you might know someone who could give an opinion on my father's tools?" she asked.

Joshua began to breathe again. He hoped that in his desire to help, he hadn't offended her.

"I could probably do it," Cooper said, looking thoughtful. "But finding a buyer who wasn't Amish is another thing. A historical re-enactor, maybe? Or one of the Hollywood outfits that film out here now and again?"

"No," she said, "if they were going to be sold to anyone, I'd prefer he was Amish. It seems more sensible, since my father collected those tools over his whole life for that specific purpose."

"You're right." Cooper nodded. "Can I give you a call in a

few days? Maybe through Joshua? We can set up a date to have a look at them."

"That sounds great," she said. "It's so nice to meet you."

"And you." And with another smile for both of them, he moved on to a pair of women admiring a painting between two of the massive windows.

"That was painted by Kiara Cooper. Come on, let's go out the back," Joshua said, resisting the urge to grab her hand and tow her through the crowd so they wouldn't be separated. Once they had their coats, his hat, and Sara's away bonnet, she followed him down a corridor, past the ranch offices, and out the rear entrance closest to the barn.

"Why didn't you tell me you wanted to evaluate *Dat*'s tools?" she asked as they went into the relative peace of the stables. "I have to say the thought never crossed my mind."

"It never crossed mine, either, until I laid eyes on John Cooper." He reached up to pat Jupiter's nose. One of the hands had brushed him down and given him some oats. "But it makes sense. Those tools would be valuable to a harness maker. If he can give you an idea of their value, you can decide better what to do with them."

"They're not doing any good to anyone at the moment, hidden in a closet," she said.

"Did I overstep?" He paused in the act of opening the stall door. "If I did, I'm sorry."

She shook her head. "No, you just surprised me. With everything that's happened, I forgot all about the tools. I hope they're still there when we go out on Tuesday."

"If they've been there for five years, they won't up and disappear the minute you get back to town," he told her. "I'm glad you're not mad at me."

Her gaze caught his. "You were trying to help. No one

could be mad about that." Then she grinned. "I appreciate your looking out for me among your high-class friends. At least I didn't have to arm-wrestle John Cooper."

He flicked her with the leading rein and she laughed.

Leading Jupiter out and hitching him up to the sleigh caused another minor ruckus as the guests tried to photograph every move, but in a few minutes the horse was pulling them briskly around the sweep and along the drive, which had been packed down by a couple dozen vehicles and would probably see a couple dozen more by midnight.

"The Madisons seem to be a nice enough family," Sara remarked. "Mostly."

"Trey is a piece of work, but I doubt he'll bother you any more."

"Believe me, unless he's on a backboard getting loaded into an ambulance, I have no intention of seeing him again at all. Is he like that with everyone? With you?"

"He tried those intimidation tactics on me when we were kids, but Chance and Clint were on my side, so he didn't get very far. He's all right once you get to know him."

"Unless you're a woman," she pointed out. "I feel sorry for his girlfriend, if he has one."

"He's had lots of them. They just don't last very long."

"Maybe you should educate him on the reason why."

"Not my business," he said. "I've got enough trouble in that department. Would you really have arm wrestled him?"

But she only laughed again. And as the sleigh's runners sang in the snow, all white and purple and streaked with gold as the sun lowered into the pines, he realized that she was far happier leaving the Rocking Diamond than she had been going toward it. And strangely, so was he.

Besides, if he'd stayed, he wouldn't have heard her laugh.

12

ON SUNDAY, Adam and Zachariah were up early in order to shovel off the front porch and stairs, while their father looked after the horses and the cows that were in the barn. Yesterday had been spent making sure the cattle out in the pastures would have enough hay for two days, but even on Sunday, it fell to Joshua to ride out and break the ice on the water tanks so that they could drink.

"Will we be able to go to church?" Sara asked Naomi as the four women got breakfast ready. This morning featured a huge frittata with curls of red and green pepper on top in honor of Christmas. Malena was frying up potatoes and onions in the cast-iron skillet, and Rebecca had just pulled the first pan of cheese-and-green-chile muffins out of the oven.

"Reuben will tell us," Naomi said calmly. "If it's too deep for the buggies, we can walk over to the bishop's and fellowship there. When you were at home, whose place did you go to when the snow was bad?"

Sara tried to think, but childhood memories had been

buried under the trauma of the accident. "I can't remember. Yoders are pretty close, aren't they?"

"A mile or so. Farther than the Wengerds are from us, but still close enough to your farm for the family to bundle up and walk." She turned to glance at the door. "I hear boots on the stairs. Best get this frittata in, Rebecca, before you put in that next pan of muffins."

After breakfast and dishes, Sara got ready for church in her new blue dress with its matching cape and apron, and did her best to wet her hair so it would lie flat long enough to get under the brim of her covering. No such luck. While the back seemed to be growing out a little, the curls in front stayed stubbornly short.

"Never mind," Malena said, popping her head into the tiny room. "By New Birth Sunday, when you're baptized, it will be long enough."

"I sure hope so." She shook her head at her reflection in the tiny hand mirror propped on the chair rail. "I guess they have to take me as they find me."

"Just like *der Herr* does," Malena told her with a smile, and clattered down the stairs.

Downstairs in Joshua's room, Sara changed Nathan and put him into his little snowsuit and knit cap, then wrapped a knitted black shawl around him for good measure. She half thought that Joshua might just stay out in the pasture until past eight o'clock, when the family would depart, but in a few minutes she heard him knocking the snow off his boots in the mudroom at the back door.

She scooted out of his room with the baby as he went in, tossing a smile over his shoulder as though he recognized the same thing she did—that sharing the room with Nathan's nanny was a finely tuned dance between privacy and necessity.

He looked after the night feedings and she took care of the daytime ones when he was out doing ranch work. When they were both in the house, she was careful to hang back. It was important for Nathan to know that Joshua was the most important person in his life. Even more important was for Joshua to bond with the baby. Naomi had been firm on that point with her daughters. "Joshua must care for him, so no running to pick him up at every cry. That's his father's job."

And now, at the end of the second week after his unexpected arrival, their strategy seemed to be working. Nathan knew his father's voice, and maybe Sara was imagining things, but it seemed that he was less fussy when Joshua bathed and changed him than when anyone else did.

Today would be Nathan's first time at church, at the tender age of four and a half months. There had been some debate about who would care for him, but Sara had spoken up. "It wouldn't really be right for Joshua to have him with the single men. I'll sit with the young mothers in the back. Everyone probably knows by now that I'm his nanny, so it won't seem strange, and it will be easier for me to slip out and take him into a bedroom if he fusses."

Naomi had glanced at Reuben, but he had made a gesture that Sara understood as, "This is for you to decide." So Naomi had nodded, and now here they were at the Yoder home, Sara making herself comfortable with the other young mothers, and trying not to feel a little strange as they cooed over Nathan. She wasn't his mother. She wasn't married. His father was with David and Philip Yoder and all the other single men outside on the porch, exchanging news until the bishop went in and it was their turn to find their places by age and sit down on the right-hand side of the room.

Had there ever been a stranger family situation in the Siksika?

Nathan lasted through the *Loblied* and into the first verses of the Christmas story from Matthew before he began to fuss. Quietly, Sara picked up the baby bag and carried him down the hall to the bedroom, where another mother was feeding her own child. The bottles in Sara's bag had been heated before they left home, and put in an insulated pouch to hold as much warmth as possible. Nathan settled to his bottle like he meant business.

Sara looked up to see the young woman watching her, and realized with a jolt that she knew her. Nearly six years older. And a few pounds heavier, after a recent pregnancy. But those brown eyes and winged eyebrows hadn't changed a bit since that night they and Lena Eicher had clutched one another in hysterics in the weeds, watching the *Englisch* boys' car disappear down the county highway into the night.

"Dinah Yoder," she whispered.

"Eicher now," Dinah whispered back. "Hi, Sara. I heard you were back. Is that…?"

"*Ja*. Joshua's boy, Nathan. He's four and a half months."

Dinah looked down at the *Boppli* at her breast, under a light blanket in case anyone should pass the door on the way to the bathroom. "This is Rosemary. Three months. My first." Her face glowed with love.

"Eicher?"

"Lena's second oldest brother. Will."

Sara wondered how that had come about. She remembered Will as a long drink of water who worked for a well outfit. Maybe Lena's family had seemed a refuge for Dinah during that terrible time. Maybe they could talk about it. And talk had led to confidences, which had led to love.

"Is Lena here?" She couldn't remember seeing her, but that didn't mean anything. There were a lot of people in the other room. She switched Nathan to her right arm and he resumed his attack on the bottle.

"*Neh*, she married a boy from Kentucky who worked on my father-in-law's place for a summer. Two years after—" She stopped.

"After the accident. It's okay, Dinah. You can talk about it if you want. Goodness knows neither of us are ever going to forget, are we?"

"That's part of why Lena was so anxious to get away. She was having nightmares. And episodes in the daytime—panic attacks, they call them."

"Same here." Sara had gone to counseling at her host family's suggestion. Two years' worth. It had been the best thing she could have done for herself. And now she hoped the *gut Gott* would do the rest. "I'm all right now."

"I hear you're going to stay. Live on the farm."

Sara nodded. "As soon as I can afford it. There's a work frolic Tuesday to help things along."

"*Ja*, my brothers plan to go."

Sara couldn't help but smile. "The Miller boys, too."

"Two of them, at least. I can't see Joshua helping out."

For some reason, this rubbed Sara the wrong way. "I think he's planning to. He's been out there a couple of times with me. And made the supply list so that everyone could divide up the cost and the tasks."

Dinah's eyebrows rose. "Is he finally going to end his *Rumspringe*, then?"

"I don't know about that." She glanced at her warm little bundle, who seemed to have finally had enough. "But he has a *gut* reason to."

"Maybe more than one."

Sara didn't know what that meant, and maybe she didn't want to know. There were some things you just didn't share with people you'd been friends with five years ago and hadn't seen since.

She put Nathan on her shoulder and patted his back until he rewarded her with some bubbles and a burp. Then, with a smile at Dinah, she packed up the bag and returned to the living room with him. The young mothers slid down to make room for her on the end of the bench. She supposed she'd do the same when the next baby's turn came.

She was able to absorb the second half of the sermon, anyway, because Nathan went to sleep after all his exertions. After the final hymn, the bishop rose to make announcements.

"I hope you are all weathering the snow. I am glad it held off long enough for us all to meet in fellowship together. I have a couple of things to say this morning, before we enjoy our fellowship meal." He glanced over his congregation and smiled, his gaze falling on Sara. "Welcome to Nathan Joshua, the newest member of the Miller family on the Circle M. And we welcome Sara Fischer back to the Siksika Valley. She is working for the Millers as the *Boppli*'s nanny."

People's clothes rustled and heads turned to see where she was sitting—first in the direction of the Miller girls, sitting with the other unmarried women, and then toward the back. Sara had never been so thankful for somewhere to look— namely at the baby, who was sleeping like a lamb and was therefore unable to give her an excuse to flee back into the bedroom.

She caught Dinah Yoder's eye by accident, and to her surprise, her former friend smiled warmly. That big, welcoming, encouraging smile from their very first day as scholars, going to the schoolhouse for the first time when everything was new and a little bit scary. Just as she had that day, she smiled back. On that long-ago day, those smiles had made them fast friends. Maybe she'd been a little hasty leaving the bedroom. Maybe she might actually still have a friend here in the valley. After all this time, and on the far side of trauma.

But Little Joe was not finished. "Sara tells me that she wishes to be baptized in the spring, so she, Malena Miller, and Rebecca Miller will begin baptism classes on January twenty-fourth, each church Sunday."

Sara looked up at the girls in surprise and delight. They hadn't said a word to her—but how wonderful that they would all be baptized together! They would be sisters in the spirit, which was as close to real sisters as Sara would ever have, now. Tears welled up, and she blinked them back before someone saw.

"If there is anyone else who would like to join these young women in their decision, please let me know by our next church Sunday."

Little Joe stepped forward into the aisle and the ministers and deacon stood, following him to the back of the room. As people rose and moved into the other rooms of the house, talking over the announcements and visiting with one another, the young men got to work moving the benches into position for the fellowship meal. Several of the young married women set the tables with plates, cups, and cutlery from the bench wagon, and when everything was ready, the two Yoder girls and several cousins brought in the food.

Before she could find a place to sit, Naomi approached her with her arms out for the baby. "You did well," she said. "Like you'd been caring for babies all your life. But I can take him now, so you can get a bite to eat."

"But I—"

Naomi smiled at her. "You'll have many old friends who will want to see you, and ask a million questions, and it's better if you have only that to think about. Nathan will be fine with me—luckily, he's sleeping, so I'll get lunch, too."

How understanding she was. Sara surrendered her charge to his *Mammi*, and when Naomi found a seat, slipped the baby bag under her place on the bench within reach. Then she joined Malena and Rebecca, who, to her astonishment, said they were saving a seat for her between them.

"Denki," she said, sliding into it. "I thought you'd be eating with your friends."

"We are," Rebecca said with a smile. It lit up a face that was usually thoughtful and abstracted. "I'm so hungry, I just want to eat everything."

After their silent grace, Sara dished up macaroni and cheese casserole with hot dogs chopped into it, and slathered peanut butter spread on a thick slice of homemade bread. There were half a dozen kinds of pickles, and in honor of Christmas, several of the woman had brought snowball salad, bristling with coconut and sweetened with apple, and Christmas jellied salad, made in three layers—green, red, and white like a snow-capped mountain.

After lunch was over, Sara and the twins helped the Yoder girls wash the mountain of dishes and box them up for Dave and Phil Yoder to take out to the bench wagon. Sara had a feeling that, while on a normal Sunday some might have gone home after the meal, today there were the additional attractions of the returned prodigal and the rebel cowboy and his unexpected baby. She had to admit, she'd have stuck around, too.

Not that people were rude. Not at all. And she only saw

cautious judgment in a few sets of eyes. But, as old Annie Gingerich told her in her cracked voice, "This is the most interesting Christmas Sunday I've seen in years, young Sara. Now, you just sit down right here and tell me where you've been."

Of course, since Annie was more than a little deaf, the entire room could hear the story. Not of that night. No one would put her through that again, especially not Annie. But the long bus ride across two states? Yes, she wanted to know about that, and more. The shedding of her Amish clothes and buying *Englisch* ones with the money *Mamm* had saved in the ginger jar on her dresser. About studying for her GED and taking the certification exams to be an EMT.

She was as open as she could be. The only thing she left out was calling the ex-Amish family's number she'd been given in a private message online. That was confidential.

When she had finished her story, Annie patted her knee. "It's all in the past, *Liewi*, past and gone, never to come again. Now you must look toward the future that *der Herr* holds for you."

She nodded and squeezed Annie's hand. "I've missed you, Aendi Annie." The little ones called her that, a term of both affection and respect.

Annie's dark eyes held her gaze. "I've missed you, too. And your family. I'm glad our loving *Gott* has brought you safely back to us. To the Siksika, where you belong."

Her old voice was so tender that Sara's eyes welled with tears.

She'd run from the valley so fast and so far that it had taken years for God to lead her around to the conviction that her place was here. Her gaze found Joshua at the back of the room, close to the stairs up to the bedrooms. What would it take for God to lead him to that place, too? How far would he have to run? And how much damage would be done to his family before he realized where his place was?

As though he had heard her questions, his lashes flicked up and his gaze met hers. She had just a moment to realize that his expression had turned to concern for her damp eyes and trembling mouth, when Nathan woke up with a start in an unfamiliar room with a crowd of unfamiliar people.

Naomi cuddled him close, tried to reassure him that he was safe and with someone who loved him. But it did no good. He shrieked, and Dinah's little Rosemary gulped and joined him. Almost as though they'd been pushed from behind, Dinah, Sara and Joshua lunged for their sobbing little bundles.

"Take him into the bedroom," Naomi advised. "He just got a fright, that's all. And he needs to be changed."

While Joshua carried his son, Sara scooped up the baby bag and they scurried into the bedroom she'd taken refuge in during the service. In ten minutes they had him changed and fresh in another sleeper. While Sara put away the soiled items to be dealt with at home, Joshua settled on the bed.

"It's all right," he said to his tearful son. "You funny little *Nachteil*, you scared a whole room full of people. How do you like that?"

Sara couldn't help a smile—Nathan's plump cheeks and rounded eyes did make him look a bit like a night owl. The baby hiccuped and his wails decreased in volume. Sara sat beside him on the bed and stroked his tiny hands with her finger. He latched on tight and his eyes widened as the two most familiar to him sat quietly, saying nonsense things until he calmed.

Joshua heaved a breath as Nathan watched him, his mouth

moving as though he were imitating the movements of his father's mouth.

"You know what they're going to think out there."

"No, what?" She tickled Nathan's cheek.

"That we're a couple."

She sat back, gawking at him a bit like an owl herself. "That's a stretch. They know I'm the nanny. Nannies are supposed to be in charge of the baby bag, aren't they?"

"I could see that look in Della Yoder's eye. I've seen it before with my brother Daniel. The whole *Gmee* had him matched up with Susan Bontrager, including Susan."

"Susan is that bossy one who wanted to hold Nathan? The previous bishop's granddaughter?"

"That's the one."

"Girl's terrified of not getting married," Sara said. "I recognize the signs. She's trying too hard."

"The point is, we're not trying at all and still it's going to start. Brace yourself."

"No problem," she said, and dropped her voice to a whisper. "No girl can compete with Seattle, and I know it."

13

No girl can compete with Seattle, and I know it.

The words whispered in Joshua's head at unexpected moments. Moments when he was honest enough with himself to wonder if they were true. Moments when he quickly stifled the urge to think about it, mostly because Nathan was crying or something needed to be done.

The next evening, when he was out in the barn making sure the animals were taken care of for the night, his phone vibrated in the inside pocket of his coat. He never had the ringer on in case *Dat* or one of his brothers were close enough to hear. He slipped it out and took refuge in the tack room, where he closed the door behind him.

"Hey, Chance," he said in a low voice.

"Hey. Just checking in to make sure your girl didn't get scared off by my knucklehead brother."

"I told you she was an EMT. Not much scares anyone in that line of work."

"Shame you guys didn't stay for the afterparty. Your friend

Tyler Carson nearly set the bunkhouse on fire trying to roast hotdogs in a wastebasket."

Joshua rubbed his forehead with his his thumb and forefinger and sighed. For this he risked being discovered with a phone by his father? "I'm sure it was hilarious."

"So listen, I called for another reason. About Plan S."

"Shhh!" Besides Tyler, Chance was the only person he'd confided in about that. *S* for Seattle. "Is anybody with you?"

"No, I'm in my room. I'm not going to give you away, don't worry. But I had an idea, which you've probably already thought of, but I thought I'd run it by you."

Chance's ideas usually involved either vehicles with a lot of horsepower or adventures that cost a lot of money, neither of which Josh could manage at the moment. "I'm listening."

"You know how you wake up in the middle of the night and you go, that's it! That's the answer. Did you ever think that maybe your girl isn't as serious as you think about living on that derelict hay farm?"

"She's not my girl," Joshua said patiently. "She's my son's nanny."

"All the better. See, I think she was too quick to dismiss Mom's offer for the farm. But Josh ... what if you could convince her to take it ... and then *go with you* to Seattle?"

Joshua sat abruptly on the chair he used when he was cleaning tack. "Are you insane?"

"It's not as crazy as it sounds. What if you could?"

"She's going to join church, Chance. They announced it on Sunday."

"That means it's written in stone?"

"Practically. Besides, she said she was out of options in Portland. That's why she came back." Because God had left her no other choice. And he would bet there was an underlying layer to it—fence jumper though he planned to be, even he could recognize the lure of the familiar, the known. Of family.

"Okay, fair enough. But what if she were only trying to talk herself into it because she *was* out of options? You have to admit, half a million dollars can give you a *lot* of options."

Free, amazing, unheard-of options that could make a whole new life for them in one fell swoop.

Them? Is that what you want? To make a life with Sara—skinny, wounded, and two years older? "But even if she did agree, we—we're not together."

"Don't you like her?"

"Well, sure. I like your brother Trey. Doesn't mean I'm going to live with him."

"Does she like your kid?"

"Yes, but—"

"You're not the first guy who got together with someone because of a baby, Miller."

"Well, yeah, but—" *Is that enough to build a life on?* "I can't ask her that, Chance. I've only known her for two weeks. She's not going to take a half-million-dollar gamble on me and my son."

"Who says it has to be both of you?" Chance demanded with maddening nonchalance. "Your mom could look after Nathan, right? I mean, he never figured into Plan S before—he doesn't have to be a complication now."

Joshua lost his breath so completely it took a couple of seconds to get it back. "What, you mean just leave him here? Walk out the door and leave him for my parents to bring up?"

"They like a big family, right?"

He tried to form words that would make sense, while the

bottom fell out of his stomach at the thought of doing such a thing. "They've raised their kids. For Pete's sake, Chance, do you want me to do to my whole family what Carey Lindholm did to me?"

"You survived, didn't you?"

"Yeah, with the help of all of them, plus a nanny!"

"Come on," Chance said, swerving away from the topic like a cheerful drunk spinning the wheel of a car. "At least float the idea past Sara about the new and improved Plan S. Then Mom gets her hay farm to put the trail riding unit of the business on, Sara gets her money, you get a life. Win-win-win."

"The trail riding unit?" Hang on. Chance was just a surprise a minute this morning. Josh was having a hard time keeping up. "You mean she doesn't want it just for a hay farm?"

"She never does one thing when she can do two, you know that. The farm apparently abuts those hills that give straight on to BLM land. There's even a lake back there, according to the survey map. It's perfect, she says. If the trail horses are over there, we can board more horses to train here, at the main stable."

It all boiled down to money. But the church had reached into its pockets to keep the taxes paid for Sara, if she ever came back. That sacrifice from many families had to mean something more than just another business unit for the Rocking Diamond.

"Would she tear down the house?" he asked, for something to fill the silence.

"Probably. She was doodling a floor plan for a stable/bunkhouse combination this morning at breakfast."

So Chance's mother was pretty certain Sara would take her offer, despite Sara's telling her she wasn't interested. It occurred to Joshua that mother and son might even have had a little conversation over coffee that had resulted in this phone call.

He wasn't sure how he felt about that. Taylor Madison had nothing to do with his life except for being the mother of his friends. It didn't feel good to have her meddling around in it, even at arms' length.

He Chance he'd think about it and stuffed the phone back into his coat. After tomorrow, he might have a better idea of how attached Sara really was to the family place. Could there possibly be a chance that she might have a secret longing to go back to the coast if she had more options? Did he even want to ask her, and give Taylor Madison the satisfaction of getting what she wanted?

He eyed the dusty old saddlebag in the wooden bin where he hid his travel things and the guidebook about Seattle. And it occurred to him that he hadn't cracked it open once since Sara and Nathan had come to the Circle M.

EARLY TUESDAY MORNING, AS HE SHOVELED DOWN HIS favorite Gold Rush Casserole, which *Mamm* made with crispy potatoes, sausage, and lots of cheese, Joshua could hardly look Sara in the eye as she brought Nathan to the table with her. Nor when she kissed the baby good-bye and climbed into the family buggy, bundled up in a warm coat and scarf, with *Dat* at the reins. He and his brothers loaded themselves into the back with their carpentry equipment and an array of shovels and axes. It was kind of a relief to be back there, where he couldn't make eye contact with her.

There were already spring wagons and buggies parked in the Fischer yard when they arrived, the horizon lightening to a glow with the sunrise. Reuben waved his crew into the house, where they gathered in the big sitting room, and Joshua set his agitated thoughts aside. Dave and Phil Yoder looked around them at the mess with the kind of expression Joshua knew he wore himself when Nathan filled his diaper.

"*Guder mariye,*" Reuben began, "and *denki* for coming out today to help our young sister remake her home so that it's livable."

"And thank you to those who contributed to the taxes so I could keep it." Sara gazed from one face to another. "I may never know who you were, but I want you to know how much I appreciate your kindness. I will pay the church back as soon as I can."

A few heads nodded, and several faces, which had been watchful at best, softened. Joshua caught himself chewing on his lip, and turned his gaze back to his father.

"So, here is the plan," Reuben went on. "We'll divide into groups. One for the house, one for the barn, and one for the land and outbuildings, which includes the water system. I'll be in that group. The house group will clean out the rooms, right down to the boards, including the cellar, and make a burn pile. We have trim boards and caulking with us, and we may need to refinish a thing or two. The barn group will muck it out and repair what is necessary. Any hay in the loft can go back out into the fields. Questions?"

"Who brought lunch?" Phil Yoder joked.

"Naomi and my girls will bring lunch at noon," Reuben said with a smile. "Don't worry, no one will go hungry for giving up a day's work on their own places."

"Which group should I go with?" Sara said.

"House," Little Joe Wengerd suggested. "The crew will want instructions on how you'd like things done."

"All right," she said, "I'll start scrubbing down walls upstairs in the bedrooms, then, and cleaning floors, if someone will caulk the windows."

The crew divided up, and Joshua walked across the yard with his father. "I'll show you where the springhouse is. I told Sara you were pretty handy with water systems."

"We've had enough practice, for sure and certain," Reuben agreed.

Josh had noticed as he went out the door that his brothers Adam and Zach, as well as Phil and Dave Yoder, were on the house crew. As the youngest of those who had come, they'd probably be delegated to the cellar. Every horrible job he'd ever had to do as punishment around the Circle M would be paid back in spades, if that were the case. His step was positively jaunty as he and his father, plus three other men, headed out through the orchard where Sara had taken refuge that first day.

It seemed like forever ago, so much had changed ... and not changed at all.

"The yard and the closest fields won't take long, Reuben," one of the men said. "I was going to suggest riding fence, but with the melt yesterday, there's no point in going out farther. It'll all just be mud, and there are no animals to keep in anyway. We'll meet you up at the springhouse with the lumber from Joshua's list in an hour or so."

Joshua hadn't expected to be alone with *Dat*. On any other day he'd be nervous. Maybe a little defensive. But today seemed different—maybe because they were both on unfamiliar land, helping someone else. Maybe they were a little more equal this morning.

Carrying shovels and a hoe, they hiked up the steep slope, passing the holding tank, until they reached the springhouse. *Dat* pushed his hat up on his head with a finger as he took it in. "*Ja,* I see what you mean. I hope our crew doesn't take its time getting up here with those boards and tar paper."

"We can get the water flowing again and the tank cleaned out in the meantime," Joshua suggested. "There's got to be five years of compost and who knows what else in there."

They went to work, *Dat* hoeing layers of autumn leaves and the evidence of long-deceased small animals out the door and Joshua shoveling the wet mass outside to be spread on the ground. It was messy work, but at the end of it, Joshua felt a sense of satisfaction at seeing the water bubble cleanly out of the spring.

Once they knew there would be water, they walked down to the next job—the holding tank.

"How big do you think this is?" Josh surveyed the tank that had been set into a cut in the hillside. The protective earth kept it warmer during the winter, which meant less likelihood of its freezing and cracking, and provided easier access than a free-standing tank. "Three thousand gallons?"

"I'd say so," *Dat* agreed. "That's the least you'd need for a family that size. The irrigation system would be separate. So, who's going in there? You or me?"

Josh snorted at what passed for his father's humor and didn't bother with an answer so obvious. He climbed up, removed the lid, clicked on his head lamp, and lowered himself in.

"All right, *mei sohn?*" *Dat* called from somewhere at ground level. "Is it dry? I've got the drain open."

"*Ja.* There's six inches of mud. Let some water in the inlet valve, would you? I'll start shoveling when it gets wet enough to flow out."

Of all the mucky, claustrophobic jobs there ever were, cleaning out a water tank ranked right up there with draining septic tanks. It took him two hours. The others arrived halfway through and handed down the portable pump and the sterilizing equipment, and at last it was done. When the head lamp revealed clean water flowing in from the pipe uphill, just as it ought, Reuben hauled him out of there with his hands under his armpits.

After Josh screwed the lid back on, the two of them sat on the top of the tank in the sun. The sound of hammering came from the springhouse up the slope as the other half of the crew repaired the little building. A couple of hardy brown sparrows balanced on the branch of a pine above, twittering at the strangers in their midst.

"I'm glad you were here," his father said. "I think I'm too old for water tanks."

"Not likely," Josh scoffed. "That's like saying a length of binder twine is too old for hay."

Dat gave a chuckle. "All the same, I'm glad we could do this together. It's been a while since you were my little helper in the tack room."

Now he pretty much managed the tack room himself. "All those hours of punishment that involved cleaning tack and oiling harness actually did me a favor," he said slowly, gazing out over the valley. "I've got a store of knowledge in my head about what well-made tack can do. What its limits are. And aren't."

Dat nodded. "It was never meant to be a punishment, Josh. I had hoped you'd develop a knack for the work."

"It felt like punishment at the time. All those fiddly pieces, cooped up in a small room when I wanted to be out racing Buttons in the field or something." And then, before his father could say it, he added, "Cutting horses aren't for racing. I know."

"Bad discipline for a highly trained animal," *Dat* agreed calmly. His gaze ranged out over the hay farm, too, resting at last on the house in the distance, a darker smudge behind it where the garden had once been. "On one hand, it will be *gut* to have someone living on this place again," he mused aloud. "But on the other hand, a girl all alone ..."

"Sara can take care of herself."

"*Ja,* but what if those rough-housers come intending to have a party, and find her there?"

With a smile, Josh told him about Trey Madison and the handshake.

Dat's eyes widened in astonishment. "Sara did that? To an *Englisch* man?"

"She didn't hurt anything but his pride. He won't bother her and risk it a second time."

"A wealthy boy like him doesn't like that, I'd imagine. I hope he doesn't take it out on her."

"Honestly, he's probably already forgotten she exists. But here's something else again—Mrs Madison offered Sara half a million dollars for this farm."

Dat jerked and Joshua grabbed him, in case he rolled off the tank altogether. "*Ischt so?* How can that be possible?"

"She wants it for a hay farm—and more. She almost bought it when the county was getting ready to put it up for sale, but the *Gmee* stepped in with the back taxes just in the nick of time."

"Joshua, you should not be telling me Sara's private business."

"How private can it be? Mrs Madison proposed it to Sara right there by the Christmas tree, in front of a hundred guests."

His father whistled, a low sound like air coming out of a tire. "What did Sara say?"

"That she had no plans to sell. But I don't know how long that will last. One good freeze and her alone in that house might change her mind."

"She grew up in that house. She knows what it's capable of, like you know your harness."

"Maybe."

"I like our Sara," *Dat* said thoughtfully. "I hope she doesn't take the Madison offer and go to another community to make her home. One where the winters aren't so hard and the growing season is longer."

"I think her mind is made up," Josh said. "She wants to stay here. I don't know how she's going to get the hay farm going again, but I'm pretty sure she'll find a way."

"I wonder if the barn crew found any equipment back there that could be refurbished?" *Dat* wondered. "Her father would have had a seeder and rake. Maybe a baler."

"If that hasn't all been carried away, I'll be surprised," Josh said. "Sara said herself it was a miracle the harness maker's tools were still in the closet where her dad kept them."

"His tools are still here?" Under the magnifying glass of his father's complete attention, Josh suddenly felt as though he were the bit of paper beginning to smoke in the beam.

"*Ja*. Two rolling chests of them. I saw John Cooper at the party and asked him if he might give her an estimate of their value."

"What for? She knows they're valuable. Even I know that. A pair of pliers or a leather punch costs fifty dollars."

"But if someone makes her an offer, it would be *gut* for her to know what she should expect. There are people all too willing to take advantage of a woman—especially one who's young and Amish."

"She may be young, but she's no ordinary Amish woman."

Josh laughed. "That's the truth." He couldn't remember the last time he'd laughed in his father's presence. The fact that they were even talking like this was a miracle on the same level as the tools' survival.

"Joshua," *Dat* said slowly, "it seems to me that the *gut Gott* is putting an opportunity in your path."

If only his father knew the whole of it. "What opportunity?"

"You know your way around tack and harness better than any of your brothers. Here are the harness-maker's tools, waiting to be used. Have you ever thought of taking up that trade yourself?"

Joshua, for the second time in twenty-four hours, was struck speechless. He gazed out over the fields below, muddy and patched with snow, the fence posts leaning this way and that and last summer's stubble on acre after acre.

The sparrows twittered again, as though remarking on the silence.

After a minute, Josh found his tongue. "Whatever made you think of that?" But he could see the line of reasoning as clear as day, from A to B and then a big jump over an empty space to C.

"The tools. And your mention of John Cooper. A man who apprenticed with him could command his own prices."

"Cooper makes saddles, and riding and cutting tack. Not buggy harness. He told me so himself at the party."

"Your knowledge would stand you in good stead there," *Dat*

said. "And I would guess that the tools to make bridles and cinches are similar to the ones used to make harness. What you didn't learn with him, you could learn from books in the library, or writing to men who do this."

"John Cooper wouldn't take me on. He must have to beat people away from his door looking to be apprentices."

"Maybe. But it wouldn't hurt to ask, if he's going to stop by the farm."

And now he felt it again, that tight feeling in his chest that he hadn't felt in a while. That trapped feeling, where his heart felt as though it didn't have room to beat. He had to turn the conversation on its back, like a turtle, to see if it could right itself.

"Is this a subtle way of telling me I may not have a job on the Circle M?"

He knew by the honest dismay in his father's face that this had been a low blow. "I would never do such a thing to my own son," he said gruffly. "But sometimes staying in one place just isn't in a man's blood. My brothers, you know, David and Marlon ... both of them didn't want to work the Circle M. They left to start their own ranches in New Mexico and Colorado. My father knew they wanted to go. He didn't try to stop them, because they would only be unhappy. An unhappy man makes mistakes and poor decisions. With cattle, as you know, a rancher can't afford to do that."

"I know." Not about the cattle. About the mistakes and poor decisions. Oh boy, did he know.

"Neh," Dat went on, "I'm simply pointing out that *der Herr* may desire a different path for you. Your love may be for ranching. And I would be nothing but pleased if it was. But it may be the craft of the harness-maker." He paused, but Josh had nothing to fill the silence with. "Goodness knows we could

use one in the district. Ordering harness from Ohio and Lancaster County and the places where people have come from can get expensive. And it takes time."

He had to say something. Even if it were just to hold things off for a little while. "I guess it wouldn't hurt to think about it," he said slowly.

Dat nodded slowly. "And see how John Cooper feels about it."

"*Ja*, maybe."

His father got to his feet and offered Josh a hand. He took it, and was pulled up the way he had been as a child and had tripped and fallen flat. *Dat* had always been there to offer him a hand. He really shouldn't deceive him like this. Get his hopes up.

But if he so much as breathed the word *Seattle*, *Dat* would go off the deep end, and life would be miserable from that moment forward. Josh would be forced to leave home and sleep in the Madison bunkhouse, or worse, leave for the West Coast without enough money for a proper start, and without time to talk with Sara about the Madison offer.

And then there was Nathan.

He could hardly believe Chance had been so cold as to suggest simply walking out the door and leaving the baby for his parents to raise. What kind of man was this person he'd called a friend? Had Joshua been so dazzled by his wealth and being included in his fast, easy life that he'd been completely blind to the empty space Chance called a heart?

But again, there was no time to think this over. Not when they had work to do. He and *Dat* scrambled down the slope that protected the water tank, and met the other half of the crew coming down with the satisfied smiles of men who had done a job well.

He took his share of the equipment and followed the group down the trail. His mind seemed to have made itself up on one front this morning, anyway. There was no way he could leave his baby boy. Come what may, no matter what path he took, he and Nathan were going to be on it together.

14

WHEN JOSHUA and his father walked in, Sara couldn't help a smile as they took in the transformation of a hard morning's work. She could barely take it in herself.

The kitchen had been stripped right down to the bare boards on the floor and the bare shelves in the cupboards. Outside in the yard was a pile of cardboard, trash, and goodness knew what else already burning, and the mattresses had been loaded on a spring wagon to go to the landfill. Another wagon held the sofa and ramshackle chairs. The house crew had even washed the walls downstairs once they'd finished carrying out everything that wasn't nailed down. She herself ached from hours of scrubbing walls, but all those buckets of dirty water had been worth it.

The past was washed away, and the future could begin with cleanliness, at any rate.

"Ischt gut," Reuben Miller said with approval, walking from the spotless but bare kitchen into the equally spotless but bare sitting room. "It feels like a different house."

"That it does," she agreed. "Every room is ready to be painted."

"I can help you with that," Dave Yoder said.

"No, I will," Joshua told him with a frown.

"I'll take you both, if you're willing," Sara said with a laugh. "You might want to be careful what you volunteer for around here."

And to her delight, a looming argument about who was going to do the most turned into a discussion of when they would do it, with the addition of Dave's brother Phil and all of the Miller boys. She felt as though *der Herr* was raining blessings down on her head.

The feeling increased when Naomi Miller and the twins arrived, driving a buggy packed with containers of food. The propane for the stove had long ago been drained and the switches turned off, so there was no sense in bringing anything meant to be eaten hot. Instead, they brought sandwiches, stuffed with turkey and dressing and cranberry jelly left over from Christmas dinner, along with several kinds of cupcakes— easy to eat standing up, since there was a table but no chairs— as well as whoopie pies and bags of potato chips. There were Thermos flasks of hot coffee and paper cups, bottles of water and juice, and even a bottle of cream for the coffee.

Though there was no heat in the house, Sara felt the warmth of good will and the kindness of her friends and brothers and sisters in the *Gmee* like a glow in her heart.

Malena carried Nathan bundled up in his basket, and as she set it on the dining table, Sara realized with surprise that he had nearly outgrown it. Malena had to tuck an errant foot back inside before she covered him with a shawl.

"You're definitely going to have to invest in a car seat," she murmured to Joshua, who was already on his second sandwich.

"And a stroller. Look how much he's grown after only two weeks."

"Hard to believe." He stuffed the sandwich into his mouth and leaned over to look into the baby's face.

"He's sleeping," Malena said. "Don't you dare wake him."

"If he's sleeping in all this racket, nothing I can do will wake him," he told his sister with a smile, and Sara could swear that Malena looked taken aback—as though her brother's smiles were as scarce as hens' teeth.

"I know you're probably all getting tired, but if we just push into the afternoon, I think we might finish everything on Joshua's list," Reuben said, polishing off a pumpkin cupcake with caramel frosting. "Can the crews tell us what they've completed?"

"Basement's empty and swept," Zach reported. "And you saw those old rat-infested mattresses out on the wagon, I expect."

"Pantry shelves were repaired," Adam said, "and we cleaned out all the cupboards, washed down the sink as well as we could considering there was only a trickle of water, and replaced the pulleys for the clothesline. You'll need new cord, though, Sara. The old one was broken in a few places."

Sara pulled her own list out of her coat pocket and made a note. Then she said, "The bedrooms were cleaned out, too, the walls and windows washed, the floors swept. Some of the house crew have volunteered to be painters—maybe Thursday?" She smiled at them, which made Phil Yoder blush and nod his head.

"The woodstove seems to be in good working order," Phil's father added. "Something hit the stovepipe pretty hard and put a bend in it, but we straightened it out and I think it will draw." He nodded toward it, dented but upright. "If you're going to paint this week, you'll need firewood to bring the house temperature up over sixty degrees. Any colder and your paint won't adhere. I'll have the boys bring you some firewood Thursday."

Sara made another note, just in case she needed to replace the stovepipe, and thanked him.

"We can't do anything about the floors just now," Phil's father went on, "and maybe not even until spring. We need warm days to open up the house and dry the finish. So let's hold off on the floors. No point taking off what finish is left on them if you're going to live here."

Sara nodded. She had no idea when she'd be able to move in—even spring seemed awfully close when there was so much to do to make the place livable again. As for its becoming a working hay farm, who knew when she'd be able to afford that?

"And the barn?" Reuben asked, as if he'd read her thoughts.

The crew's faces wrinkled with a disgust that practically told the story. "You'll have to get a professional to clean the manure pit," one of them said. "It's not safe for a man to go down there. The milking pen was busted up for firewood, looks like, so we pretty much made a new one. Hay loft is cleared of a lot of moldy hay and re-floored. Horse stalls mucked out and scrubbed down."

"Equipment?" Joshua asked. "Anything left?"

"For a wonder, there was," said another man. "We found the seeder under a pile of hay. Birds and rodents had got to all the seed, of course. But no windrow rake. No baler either. There's a harrow, but it must have belonged to your *Grossdaadi*." He smiled at Sara. "Those rusty old tines would probably snap if you stuck them in the soil." He looked at the ceiling, as though trying to remember if there was anything else. "Oh, and we found a plow," he added. "Nothing wrong with it except there's no rig to harness it to a horse. Rodents got it, right down to the buckles."

"That's more equipment than we expected," Reuben said to Joshua. "A seeder is *gut*. Gives a few months' grace if we can put in an early crop and get some money coming in. *Denki*, all of you," he said to the room at large. You've done well. Let's button things up this afternoon. My boys and I will get the water going in the house. Now that the tank is filling, we don't want the pipes to freeze."

Sara had been worried that the buried pipes would have frozen and cracked. Digging them up would be another expense—she couldn't very well ask the men to come back for that job, so she would have to hire an outfit to do it. The very thought of how much money all this was going to cost overwhelmed her as she walked slowly into the bathroom to find her rubber gloves.

When all the pipes in the house had been carefully inspected, Reuben deemed it safe to turn on the water and see what happened. Sara came out into the kitchen to watch, as though it were a ceremonial occasion. With nowhere else to sit, Malena perched on the kitchen table, Nathan in her arms sucking energetically on a bottle. Naomi and Rebecca worked around her, putting away the last of the food.

"Here goes." Joshua opened the faucets in the kitchen sink and a shower of mud and dead leaves came out.

"Oh no!" After all the wonderful things that had been given her today, Sara had dared to hope she might escape some horrible disaster. It looked like she wouldn't be that lucky.

"It's all right," Joshua assured her over his shoulder. "The water pressure is flushing out the pipes and any mud from the holding tank up the hill. Just give it a minute."

Hardly daring to breathe lest the water suddenly dry up, Sara watched the muddy mess run into her clean sink.

"What we don't want to see is the pressure dropping to a trickle," Reuben said. "That will mean there's a leak somewhere in the pipes."

But the pressure didn't drop, and within a few minutes, the water was flowing clear into the sink.

The Yoder boys cheered, and even Reuben grinned with triumph.

"I think it's all right," he said. "Once you get the propane hooked up again, you'll have hot water, too."

The water ceremony seemed to signal that the bulk of today's work was done. It was getting on for two o'clock, and many had their own animals and families to look after before darkness fell. Sara stood at the door and thanked every man who had come. She would never forget this. Every time she turned on the faucet, she would think of mud spewing out of it and the men who had taken such care to clean and repair the springhouse and tank up the hill until it ran crystal clear again.

"We'll see you Thursday, Sara," the Yoder boys said as they went out with their father. Phil added, "The hardware store doesn't open until eight—meet you there to choose your colors."

"I'll be there and glad to see you all," she assured him, and the poor young man blushed again.

"Better watch that one," Naomi said in a low tone, passing her in the doorway with a plastic tub full of food. "I think he's sweet on you."

Sara couldn't help making a derisive sound. "Hardly. He doesn't even know me."

But Naomi only laughed as she made her way out to the buggy.

By three o'clock, she had scrubbed down the bathroom with the help of faucets and taps that worked. Such a miracle running water was! And that was the last task that they could do today, at least. Somehow it worked out that the whole Miller family went home in the big family buggy, leaving behind the smaller one in which his mother and sisters had come. Hester waited patiently between the rails.

"I think we've been set up." At the front window, she watched the Miller buggy trundle off down the lane. Sara held Nathan in his little snowsuit, which was already feeling quite snug on his body. "How convenient that you and I get to drive home together."

"Oh, sorry," he said, coming out of the kitchen looking startled. "I told them to go. I thought you'd want a walk-through to see it all."

"I do," she said, deciding that moment that it was a good idea. "It was good to hear what everyone had done, though."

"Well, come on." He held out his arms for the baby. Nathan went into them without so much as a squeak, and settled against his father's shoulder. "Someone's ready for a tour." He kissed the baby's cheek.

Sara tried not to fall over with astonishment. Surely he couldn't have missed him that much after only a few hours? She watched him as they walked through the house, he making comments about what could be done and she writing it down on the growing list in her pocket. Even in the cellar, he took the steps carefully so as not to jiggle the baby too much.

Wonders never ceased.

She plucked the woollen shawl out of the basket as they went out the back door, heading for the barn. "Here. The wind is cold."

Instead of wrapping the baby in it, he shook his head. "You

take it. I'll put him inside my coat."

So they were both snug and warm as they walked through the barn, which still looked old and battered, but was at least clean and organized.

"I can hardly believe so much got done in only a day," she marveled as Joshua inspected the seeder and the few other pieces of equipment. "I can never repay them."

"We've raised a barn in only a day," he pointed out. "At least this one was already built."

She had to smile. "True. But I'll offer to reimburse the Yoders for the paint, at least. That's not going to be cheap."

"It's up to you, but I think you'll find they'd rather take off that hay crop for you. It would be a *gut* exchange." With Nathan against his chest, Joshua leaned against the post of one of the stalls. Not so much as a cobweb hung above his head, it was so clean. "That is, if you really do plan to move here and get the farm working again."

She sighed, pulled the shawl more snugly around her shoulders, and leaned her sore shoulders against the wall next to him. "That is the plan. But my goodness, the sheer amount of money it's going to take is overwhelming. The least stressful step is getting the propane tank filled. At the other end, there's buying a buggy horse and a used buggy. A couple of field horses. A baler and the other equipment." She scrubbed her face with the ends of the shawl. "And that's just outside. Meanwhile, there's nothing to sit on or sleep in—not so much as a facecloth to wash with. My brain is going to explode at the thought of it all."

"Don't do that," he teased. "The barn crew will be upset if you make a mess."

The rascal had surprised a smile out of her. "You always know how to keep me from spinning off into a fit, don't you?"

"You've kept me from a few bad choices, too." He was silent a moment, then looked up at her. "There's always the other option."

"What, taking Mrs Madison's offer?" She didn't pretend to misunderstand, and leaned her head back on the wall behind her. "Don't think I haven't thought about it. Repeatedly."

"But you told her no at the party."

"I know, and I meant it. But wouldn't it make things so easy? Just take the money and buy one of those loft apartments over the shops in Mountain Home. Work for the fire department. Go to church on Sundays. What a life."

"Ja," he said. "But?"

"But that would be spitting in the eye of the *Gmee,* wouldn't it? After all they've done—not only today, but also keeping the taxes paid, just on the off chance I'd come back."

"The property was used—the hay was harvested, the house rented. It didn't just sit here waiting for you."

"I know, but your father said they wanted to keep it in Amish hands. My hands."

"You don't have to do what my father wants."

Now she turned to stare at him. "Isn't it my place to obey? To listen to the *Gmee* and try to fit in?"

"It's not them looking at a lifetime of work on this place."

"Oh, come on, Josh. Every family in the valley has a lifetime of work on their place. It's the Amish way, to work close to the land. To stay grounded and humble. Even if you have a shop in town. Right?"

"Ja, but not every family has the choices you do."

"What's that supposed to mean?" She examined the set of his jaw. "I can see in your face you want to say something, but you don't know how I'll react."

"I don't want your brain to explode," he said, trying to joke about it, which only cemented her conviction that there was something on his mind. Something serious.

"Spit it out," she said.

"Well, by a huge coincidence, I was talking to Chance Madison last night."

She smacked the boards behind her, and Nathan stirred at the sudden sound. "I knew it. I knew there was something more. What did he say?"

"When I said *coincidence*, I meant not a coincidence at all. His mother is dead serious about the offer. They want to get the hay farm going again, but they also want to move the trail riding business over here. Seems this property abuts the BLM land up over the hill. Perfect for trail riding."

Sara stared at him. "You don't say. And isn't she well informed."

"Just a mother-son heart-to-heart over breakfast. With a survey map involved."

"Good grief." Taylor Madison knew more about her property than she did. "You told him I wasn't interested, right?"

With a nod, he went on, "And he suggested something else. Something that made me think. And the more I thought, the more disgusted I got."

Sara braced herself mentally, and made sure her shoulders lay against the boards once more.

"He suggested that when you sold to the Rocking Diamond, you and I and Nathan should take the money and make a new life together. In Seattle."

She wondered if her knees would hold her up while she got her lungs working again. "What a good friend, looking out for you like that," she said finally. "Nathan, too, huh?"

"Actually, he suggested I dump Nathan on my parents and just leave, but I'd never do that."

Her mouth opened, but this time, no words came out at all. Until she managed, "His idea of a good plan is child abandonment? I think you need to pick better friends."

"*Ja,* maybe so."

"Maybe? Are you kidding? Now *I'm* disgusted."

"Would running off with me and half a million dollars be so bad?" He gazed up into the rafters of the barn, as though he were asking a rhetorical question. Making a joke. Which he couldn't be.

Could he?

Sara's brain ground to halt. It took a minute for the gears to mesh and start up again. "Joshua, are you proposing to me?"

"I didn't say anything about marriage. If we were in Seattle, we wouldn't have to get married. Just buy a nice house and live there, the three of us. I'd get a job and—"

"I hate to break it to you, but half a million dollars won't even buy a condo in Seattle. It'll barely buy a mailbox. And while we're talking numbers, here's a few for you. One, I'm not going to live with anybody without a serious commitment like marriage. Two, I'm not going to break your parents' hearts. And three, what kind of man thinks flitting off to the coast with someone else's money and no commitment is a good idea? I don't want to be anybody's roommate and fund a comfy life for him. I want to build a home and be someone's lifelong love!"

He stared at her, evidently struck silent. Nathan gave a little gasp, as though he were about to cry.

"You tell your friend Chance Madison that there is no way in eternity I'll ever sell to the Rocking Diamond." She pushed herself off the wall. "And you can take your lukewarm, no-feelings-attached, ridiculous attempt at a proposal and—and throw it in the manure pit!"

Her boots sounded hollow as she stomped down the wide currying corridor into the bigger space of the barn.

"Sara, wait! I didn't mean to offend you!"

"Well, you did!" she shouted over her shoulder.

He couldn't move as fast without joggling the baby, but he followed her out at a fast walk and even rolled the big barn door shut behind him.

"Wait!"

She couldn't wait to get away from him. From the sudden knowledge that while she had actually begun to think they were becoming friends, learning to understand each other, and —on her side at least—developing the first tiny green shoots of feelings, he had obviously had something quite different in mind. If the property hadn't been in the equation, would he have asked her to run away with him? If she came just as she was—flat broke and without an asset to her name but her own brain?

Ha! Now she knew how Jane Eyre felt when she suddenly came into money and just as suddenly got an offer of marriage. And with as little emotion attached!

Joshua caught up to her as she was locking the back door of the farmhouse, with its new lock and plywood over the broken pane, and tried to apologize. All she said was, "Give me the baby."

And when she refused to say another word all the way back to the Circle M, he finally fell silent. He let her off at the steps up to the house. Then put Hester and the buggy away.

At least, she assumed he did. Because she never saw him at dinner, nor for the rest of the night.

Fine. She hoped he had gone to the Rocking Diamond to deliver her final refusal to the Madisons. Maybe he'd even stay there.

❧ 15 ❧

THE NEXT MORNING, the *Englisch* taxi—a white van driven by a middle-aged woman with a Chihuahua in the front passenger seat—rolled up the lane to fetch Naomi and Nathan for their respective medical appointments.

When she'd called, Sara had said they'd have a new baby along, so to Naomi's relief, there was a baby seat waiting for Nathan when they climbed in.

"Hallo, Sharlene," Naomi greeted her cheerfully, while Sara strapped the baby in as though she'd done it a hundred times. Maybe she had, in those five years away.

"Hallo, Naomi," Sharlene said, looking over her shoulder. "Who's this little one?"

"His name is Nathan. He belongs to my youngest son, Joshua. His girlfriend left him with us permanently, so we're taking him for his checkup today."

Sharlene's eyes widened. "Not that Lindholm girl."

"Afraid so." Sara climbed into the seat on the door side, leaving Nathan in the middle between the two of them. "This is Sara, Nathan's nanny. Sara, Sharlene Mackenzie. And Papita, of course."

"Nice to meet you, Sharlene." Sara leaned around the passenger seat. "And who's a good doggo, hey? Is it Papita?"

The little dog yapped happily, then settled into her seat as Sharlene turned the van around and headed down the lane, then turned south toward Libby. They talked of the weather and the likelihood of more snow before New Year's. Of the Lindholms and what a shame it was that they'd raised such an irresponsible daughter—Sharlene lived on the street behind them.

"I heard your boy visited the Lindholms to offer them custody, and they kicked him out," she said, passing a logging truck.

Naomi stared at the woman via the rear view mirror, but Sharlene was focused on getting around the truck. This was the first she'd heard of it. Her skin had gone cold with horror. Her son? Offer those *Englisch* people custody of their little Nathan?

"Where did you hear that?" Sara asked with a glance at Naomi. "We didn't tell anyone."

"My sister lives across the street from them and saw the whole thing. Well, the kicking out part, anyway." She cackled with glee. "And she saw that slick Lindholm pitch a fit when he stepped in the horse apples behind his car. Serves him right for looking at his phone instead of where he was going."

Sara put her hand over her mouth, but Naomi was not smiling. "When did this happen?" she asked the girl.

"The day after he came," she said, sobering instantly.

"And you didn't think to tell us?"

Sara shook her head. "I'm sorry, Naomi. I thought that if Joshua wanted you to know, he'd tell you. And there wasn't much to tell, in the end." She leaned over to kiss the baby. "Was there, sweet boy?"

Naomi couldn't think about what that said about Joshua, as quick to give up his child as ever Carey Lindholm had been. She put her hand on her belly, which was beginning to roll from the curves in the road. "Sharlene, could you slow down just a bit? I think I might be getting carsick."

"Oops, sorry. It won't be long now. We're coming up on the outskirts of town."

At the little complex of medical offices, Naomi arranged with her to be picked up in ninety minutes, and the van drove off.

"I'm sorry, Naomi," Sara said in the courtyard, the baby in her arms. "I didn't want to say in front of Sharlene, but the Lindholms don't want him. Don't even want to know him. They threatened to sue us for slander, for Pete's sake, if we said any more about it."

"Slander?"

"Yes. Gossiping about them. Which clearly everyone in the neighborhood already is."

Naomi couldn't stop the words from spilling out of her mouth. "But Joshua—how could he? Offer his own child to those *Englisch* people?"

"Well, they are Nathan's grandparents, too. Josh thought they would want to know. So he offered them joint custody. Like they could take him on weekends and every other holiday, that kind of thing. It seemed the sensible and compassionate thing to do, at least from where I stood. But Mr Lindholm called us a pair of crooks and kicked us out of the house."

Naomi found she could breathe again, and that terrible crushing burden on her spirit seemed to lift. "Joint custody. He wasn't trying to give Nathan away."

"No." Sara frowned. "As mad as I am at him at the moment, I don't think he would ever do that. In fact, he told me—" She stopped herself. "—something that makes me pretty sure he wants to be a real father to Nathan. For good."

"I'm glad to hear it," Naomi said, wondering what those unsaid words had been. "Well, let's go in or they'll think we aren't coming at all."

Sara went off to the pediatric side of the building, and Naomi was ushered into her doctor's office.

"Well, Mrs Miller," Dr Gupta said with a smile. "It's been a while since I've seen you."

For sure and certain, it must have been—there were silver threads in the doctor's hair that hadn't been there last time. But her smile was still as kind, her eyes as warm as the first day Naomi had met her and given her trust without hesitation.

"What brings you here today?" She settled into her chair as if for a good chat, and Naomi wiggled a hip up on the examination table.

"Mostly that I couldn't convince my husband I didn't need to come," she said wryly. "He was close to his grandmother, you see, and when she died of stomach cancer, he grieved a long time. Every time the children get a stomach ache or I throw up, he's convinced we're all going to die the same way."

"Poor man. I hope your thriving health convinces him eventually. But what's this about throwing up?"

Naomi told her about all the trouble she'd had a few months ago, and how even today she'd had a small bout of carsickness. "But that's probably because I haven't been in a car in ages," she said hastily. "I feel fine now."

"Do me a favor and get on that scale, would you?"

Naomi took off her shoes—every little bit helped—and

steadfastly refused to look at the weights as they slid along the rail.

"Hm. You've gained a bit. Ten pounds or so."

"It's Christmas. You should have seen the size of our dinner on Friday. And it was church Sunday, too."

The doctor asked some more questions—about her general health, about the vitamins she took, about exercise. That was a good one—as if any Amish woman needed more exercise when simply managing a household and keeping it clean was a workout every single day. Then she asked her to pee in a cup. Naomi couldn't see the reason for it, but she wouldn't dream of disobeying. When she came back, a package was already opened on the instrument table, waiting for the cup. There was nothing wrong with Naomi's eyes. She could read the label from where she sat.

"Doctor, what— That can't be for me."

Dr. Gupta simply dipped the stick in the cup, waited a minute, then raised it so that Naomi could see. "It's blue. That means you're pregnant, Mrs Miller." That warm smile dawned like a sunrise. "Congratulations."

Naomi's mouth fell open and her mind went completely blank. The only words that came out were, "I don't have stomach cancer?"

The doctor was kind enough not to laugh. "No, indeed. If you'd like, we can do a sonogram to see exactly how far along you are. And I'd like to do a pelvic exam, too. With your healthy body, there's no reason you shouldn't have a baby, but I'm going to keep a close eye on you all the same."

"P-pregnant?" Naomi's mind finally got working again. "I can't be pregnant. I'm forty-nine years old!"

"And you're physically fit, with your weight in the range it should be. A little over, but not enough to worry about. The test doesn't lie. Do you have time for the other examinations, or would you rather come back?"

"The weather won't hold forever." How prosaic she sounded when her world had just done a somersault! "Best do it all now."

The result was a bit of discomfort and a glossy picture of a bunch of gray and white lines and shapes that Naomi couldn't understand. "I've never had one of these before. What am I looking at?"

"You're about five months along and—"

"Five months!" She'd been in *der familye weg* for five months and never suspected a thing! Never even thought to wonder where her monthly had gone, what with Daniel and Lovina falling in love, and the bustle of getting the cattle off to market, and then the grand surprise of Nathan. What was wrong with her that she'd forgotten the signs that had once been so very familiar?

"Yes," Dr Gupta said. "The baby looks healthy, and so do you." Her finger moved over the lines and shapes. "This is the head, the arms, the legs. Do you want to know whether it's a boy or a girl?"

"Yes," Naomi said. No point in delaying the surprise when today was the surprise to end all surprises.

"It's a girl. See, here?"

It was difficult to see, but if Dr Gupta saw a girl, then it was a girl. Naomi felt a rushing kind of glow as her shock dissolved into pure joy. "A girl," she breathed, holding the picture with both hands. "I'll have three girls and four boys. Oh, won't the twins be happy!"

"Everyone will be—"

"Oh my goodness!" she exclaimed.

"Did you feel a kick?" Dr Gupta sat forward. "You should start feeling those around this time."

"No, I didn't. I only meant— My son is a new father. His boy Nathan is nearly five months. These babies will be so close in age!"

Dr Gupta laughed. "Nathan will have a little auntie younger than himself. Not too many children can say that, can they?"

And suddenly, Naomi was laughing and crying, and the doctor was pulling her into a hug, and her world rocked back on to its axis once again. *Der Herr* was surely smiling, too, having given her this unexpected gift. She could hardly wait to get home to tell Reuben.

She waited in the glassed-in courtyard for Sara, pulling the sonogram out of her purse now and again to look at it. Another *Dochder*, after twenty years. Wouldn't it be lovely to call her after Reuben's *Mammi*, when he'd been so worried? "Deborah Miller," she murmured. "Oh, I like that."

The sound of crying preceded Sara out of the pediatric wing. "I hope Sharlene comes soon—Nathan did not like the doctor manhandling him one bit. I've been walking him up and down while I waited for you. What have you got there, Naomi?"

Wordlessly, Naomi handed the sonogram to her and Sara took it with her free hand.

Then she sat beside her with a thump on the slatted bench. "You're pregnant?" she said. "That's why you've been feeling sick?"

Nathan roared, the sound bouncing off every hard surface in the little courtyard.

"Yes," Naomi replied, completely unable to keep the smile

off her face. "It's a girl. Five months along. Come on, Nathan. Come to *Mammi* and see if that helps."

She'd hold another baby just like this in four more months! A spring baby. What a miracle!

"Congratulations," Sara said, and gave them both a hug. "You look delighted."

"I am. You're the first to know. Oh, I wish Sharlene would hurry up. I want to tell Reuben."

"Don't we have errands to run?"

But Naomi shook her head. "Not today. I want to go home and share this with the family. There, now. Nathan just needed a change of scenery."

The roars were decreasing in volume. And then Sharlene pulled up in front of the steps and waved. "Not a word, now. Sharlene is the nicest woman in the world, but every word goes in the ears and out the mouth."

"Understood," Sara said.

Nathan fell asleep on the way home, and Naomi couldn't help but follow his example. She woke with a start when the van's front tire fell into the pothole at the gate of the Circle M. Every year they filled it, and every winter it formed again.

Reuben came to the door of the barn and stood waiting, taking off his gloves. She could tell by the tension in his body that he dreaded the news from the doctor. She paid Sharlene and then, while Sara carried Nathan into the house for the rest of his nap, Naomi hurried over to her husband.

He took her hand and led her into the barn, redolent with the smell of the hay he'd been forking to the cows and horses. He stopped at one of the horse stalls, where long ago they'd come to a sweet understanding that had led to a marriage and six children.

Seven.

"Well?" he said hoarsely.

She went into his arms like a homing pigeon. "I'm in *der familye weg*," she said, smiling into his eyes. "Five months. It's a girl."

She felt him stagger, as though his knees had gone out for a second. "Expecting? You're *expecting?*"

"*Ja*. Isn't it wonderful?"

He didn't answer right away. But his chest heaved as though he'd run the quarter mile down the lane.

"Reuben, aren't you happy about it?"

"*Ja,* of course," he said, sounding dazed. "A *Boppli*. A girl. They know these things now?"

"I could show you a picture, but you wouldn't make heads or tails of it. I can't. But the doctor can, and that's what she said."

"But Naomi—will you be safe? At forty-nine, is it all right?"

And now she saw the source of his hesitation. "There's nothing preventing me from having a baby safely. You're not to worry. Things are different now than they were even when we had Joshua. The doctor is going to see me once a month, just to keep an eye on me, she says."

With a long sigh, the tension went out of him, and his arms went around her with conviction. "I'm so happy," he said against her *Kapp*. "A girl!"

"I thought we might call her after your grandmother. Deborah."

His chest hitched, and his cheek next to hers became hot with his emotion. "I think that would be *wunderbaar*. Ah, Naomi, I love you so much."

"And I love you, even if you're a worrywart." She kissed him, and felt the moisture of a tear on his cheek as her lips left his. "Two *Bopplin* in the house come spring. I never thought I'd see the day."

"The *gut Gott* has truly blessed us," he whispered. "Ever since the night you kissed me first, right here."

She did it again, a stolen peck, just as she had nearly thirty years before. "Come. Let's tell the children they're going to have a sister."

Hand in hand, they walked through the barn. As they passed the closed tack room door, Reuben guessed her thoughts. "*Ja,* Joshua is home. I don't know what happened between him and Sara, but he spent the night at Tyler Carson's in town."

"Better there than the Rocking Diamond."

"I agree. Did she say anything to you about a quarrel?"

"I wouldn't have wanted her to in Sharlene's van, but no."

He was silent. "Does she confide in you?"

"Not yet. Not about important things. But Joshua seems to be opening up to you, which gladdens me."

"Maybe he will about this, too. I hope so. Our boy is carrying the burden of a choice. I wish I could do something—say something—to help him. Our talk yesterday was so *gut,* but I don't want to horn in on his confidence again in case I spoil it."

Naomi knew full well how prickly and unhappy her youngest son was. "I think Nathan will be the making of him. We may find him growing up now in a way he hasn't before. In mind. And in spirit."

"I pray so, every day, out there on horseback."

"And we know *der Herr* favors those prayers above all others," Naomi teased, with another smacking kiss.

Then, together, they went into the house to tell the children.

❧ 16 ❧

SARA HAD SEEN Joshua's face when his parents had shared their happy news over supper the night before. The shock—the smile—and then a kind of stillness, as though a thought had occurred to him that needed thinking over. It hadn't surprised her a bit when he'd gone out to the barn. Or when he hadn't come back in.

A surprise was waiting this morning, when seven o'clock came and he was not only back, he had already harnessed Hester to the spring wagon. They were waiting for her when she came down the steps.

"I wasn't sure you'd come with me," she said, sliding the door closed as he clucked to Hester and they moved out. "I was going to ask Adam to help me hitch up."

"Why wouldn't I come with you?" He glanced at her curiously.

"Um, because we had a little dustup on Tuesday and you've been gone ever since?"

"You mean, you had a temper tantrum and shouted at me, and I laid low to give you some space."

"I did not have a temper tantrum!" she exclaimed, resisting the urge to punch him on the arm. "I reacted like any woman would at being treated like a sugar mama."

Joshua rolled his lips inward and seemed to bite them. Then he said, "I don't know what that is."

"The female version of a sugar daddy. Someone who bankrolls another person in exchange for ... favors and services."

"Oh. Well, you're getting services, I guess. Painting, water, you name it. And I'm not asking for a thing."

That was true. He had done nothing but help her, and she had yelled at him for an idea that hadn't even been his to start with. Sara began to feel as though she might have overreacted just a little. "You weren't really serious about that, were you? The whole *let's be a family in Seattle* thing?"

He turned south on the county highway and Hester picked up her pace.

"No, I guess not. I felt it was only fair to tell you it was an option, but I never thought you'd take it. A person needs to know all their options, even if they're only going to take one."

"And now you have another one, don't you?"

Again that curious glance. "What do you mean?"

"Well, with a little *Schweschder* coming."

He shook his head like a horse would shake off a fly. "I don't follow."

Maybe she should just keep her mouth shut and not give him any more ideas. But she'd put her foot in it now. "In the interest of laying all a person's options on the table, I just thought that now that there's going to be another newborn in the house in a couple of months, it wouldn't be so hard to leave Nathan behind. Your *Mamm* and *Schweschdere* will be all about baby care, whether it's one or two."

Silence fell, punctuated by the clip-clop of Hester's hooves on the pavement.

"Tell me you didn't mean that." His face had gone stiff.

"It's an option," she quoted back at him.

He turned to her, and the fire in his gray eyes made her skin go cold. "One, as you would say, I would never leave Nathan behind. And two, have you been the one talking to Chance now?"

"No, but things have changed," she said. Now she was the one who deserved the punch on the arm.

"Not that much," he said, shaking his head in disgust. "I can't believe you think I'm just the same as Chance Madison."

"I know you're not, Joshua."

"You could have fooled me."

"Stop repeating the things he says to you, then, like some kind of ventriloquist's puppet." Oh, why couldn't she keep her mouth shut?

"I told you already why I said that. It's an option. You refused it. Leaving Nathan here with another baby in the house is an option. I refused it." He glared at her. "Now we're even. Are we done with our options?"

"*Ja,*" she said. "*Ja,* we're done. I'm sorry I brought it up."

He was silent for a moment. "And I am sorry I said that. About Seattle. I never would have dreamed that up on my own, believe me."

"Did you stay at the Rocking Diamond the other night?"

He shook his head. "I can't look at any of the Madisons right now. I walked into town and stayed at Tyler's."

"You didn't have to leave home in the dead of night because of me."

"I needed to walk it off. Do some thinking. It was all right."

She touched his woolen coat sleeve. "Are we okay?"

He appeared to consider it, then he nodded.

Something inside her, that had been wound as tight as a clock spring, relaxed. She inhaled a deep breath of cold air into lungs that worked again.

"Aren't you going to ask me what I was thinking about, walking down the highway?" he asked.

"I'm afraid to, in case you make me get out."

He smiled, and there was that dimple again. So distracting. She looked ahead, to where the outskirts of Mountain Home lay in the distance. Another mile left to go. Another mile of actually talking.

"I was thinking about Seattle."

Her heart gave a kick, but she kept her tone level. "As you do."

"As I do, and I was wondering why I'm not in the all-fired hurry to get out there like I was even a month ago."

"You have this little anchor that weighs about twelve pounds, for one thing."

"Right, but he's very portable. So there has to be something else."

"Your cranky nanny who blurts out everything on her mind whether or not anyone wants to hear it?"

"Maybe. Sometimes my cranky nanny is nice, though." He pushed out his lower lip as though he might take it back. "Sometimes."

Sara elbowed him in the ribs.

"I think it's because I didn't realize I had options right here in the Siksika. Other than the ranch, I mean. I didn't tell you what *Dat* suggested to me up there on the hillside. When we were cleaning the water tank."

"A lot of stuff has happened," she reminded him. Like a big

fight and a pregnancy. "We haven't actually been speaking. What did he say?"

"He thinks I should talk to John Cooper about apprenticing with him as a harness maker."

A silence fell again, but this time it was the silence of sheer astonishment. And Joshua, being Joshua, didn't break it. He let the idea sink in. Because there was only one reason he considered this one of his options at all. "My father's tools."

"Partly," he admitted. "I couldn't afford to buy them from you. *Dat* says one pair of pliers or a punch can run fifty dollars new. We'll know more if Cooper stops by to give you a value on them."

Her mind raced. The young man who spent half his time in the tack room was an obvious choice for such a craft. But—

"So ... you'd stay in the valley? Not go to Seattle?"

"It's an—"

"—option." He gave half a smile as they said the word together.

They were coming to the first of the houses on the north side of Mountain Home. Their time for private conversation before they reached the hardware store was running out.

"I suppose it depends on what Cooper says," he went on. "I told *Dat* he probably had a line of men out the door, all wanting to be his apprentice. My chances aren't good, especially if I soak up what he can teach me and then leave to start my own business."

"Not if you're honest about it," she said. "There's nothing wrong with training for your own shop. People don't expect their apprentices to work for them forever, do they?"

"No. And you're right. I'll tell him what I'd like to do, and see what he says. If it's no, then maybe I can learn from books and things."

"Like I would do if I were to be a *Dokterfraa*." She nodded. "It's possible. Maybe not the easiest road, but certainly possible." She smiled. "We can study together at the table, like we used to do when we were little scholars."

He laughed and pulled up in front of the hardware store, where the Yoder wagon was already waiting out front.

As she hopped out, she realized she hadn't asked the most important question of all. In all this talk of options, was there room for a change of heart? The kind that led to joining church and finding a wife?

Sara knew she had courage—had proved it a time or two when faced with a burning building and a person who needed help. But for all her bravery, she didn't have enough to ask those questions.

SARA HAD NEVER KNOWN HOW MUCH FUN CHOOSING PAINT colors could be. The Yoder boys and Joshua would suggest the most appalling pinks, purples, and oranges, and she would laugh at their jokes and choose what she'd already decided. Butter yellow for the kitchen and the spare room downstairs, and a gray as pale as a hazy summer day for the sitting room and bathroom. The wainscoting and chair rails, of course, would be creamy white, just as they had once been when *Mamm* had decided such things. As for the upstairs bedrooms, she stuck to her decision there, too. A green so pale it was nearly white, only shown up because of the white trim.

"The buds on the trees look like that just after their blushing stage, when they're just leafing out," she told the boys, who rolled their eyes at her fanciful talk. "It looks like a green mist in the woods, not individual leaves at all."

They could roll their eyes if they wanted to, but they

handed over the money for her choices all the same, and loaded the cans of paint, brushes, and trays into the Circle M spring wagon.

The Yoder spring wagon was full of firewood, and at the farmhouse, the young men wasted no time kindling a fire in the kitchen woodstove, then opening up every inside door in the house to warm the rooms before they began. Drop cloths went down. Ladders clattered. And then the crew got started downstairs. Painting the rooms and bringing them back to an all-new life gave Sara even more pleasure. And by the time they unpacked the hamper she had put in the back of the spring wagon for lunch—once again, eaten standing up—the whole downstairs had been completed, even to the window trim.

"What about the kitchen door?" Dave Yoder went to the back door and opened it to assess its condition. Then something caught his attention. "Hey, Sara, come look at this."

Sara joined him, half expecting more beer cans to have been lobbed at the door when someone couldn't get in.

Four ladder-back chairs stood in a neat row on the porch.

"What on earth?" she said, her voice rising to a squeak of surprise. "Joshua, did you bring these?"

"Not me," he said around his chicken salad sandwich. "Are those yours? From before?"

"I don't know. They could be. Lots of families have those chairs," she said. "There was a big going-out-of-business sale at the furniture store when I was a kid, and everybody got as many as they could, for the older folks at church and for family holidays and things."

"Well, let's bring them in. I could use a chair."

"Four people on the painting crew, four chairs," Phil said

with satisfaction, pulling one of them up to the table. "Considerate. Cold, though."

"That's not all," Dave said as he brought in the last one. He gestured over his shoulder with his chin. "There's a box."

Sara went outside to collect it, set it next to the hamper on the table, and opened its flaps. She lifted out wadded-up newspaper that would help start the stove the next time, and let out a long breath. "Well, for goodness sake." The boys peered into the box while Phil took another sandwich out of the hamper without even looking. "It's the clock *Dat* gave *Mamm* when they got engaged. From the *Eck*. I don't understand."

She lifted it out. It had stopped ages ago, of course. The key was taped to the underside so she wound it, then carried it into the sitting room. She opened the freshly cleaned glass doors of the *Eck* cabinet and set it in its old place on the shelf second from the top, at eye level. The balls turned and flashed. "Someone even polished it before they brought it over."

"Maybe some things went for safekeeping," Joshua said, "and weren't looted, like we thought."

"Maybe," she said. "But my goodness, when? I just walked out the door with my stuff in a couple of canvas grocery bags because we didn't have a suitcase. Just left everything where it stood. The church must have rented it fully furnished."

"*Ja*, Rose Stoltzfus and her family did," Dave said. "Alden said it was a good thing, because they didn't have very much. But they've been in their own place a long time, after he opened the smithy."

"Don't suppose we'll ever know," Phil said, peering into the hamper. "Did you bring any of those cupcakes?"

"Under the bags of chips," she said absently. "I'd sure like to thank them, whoever they are. This clock was the one thing

I grieved when I saw it was gone. *Mamm* loved her clock. Treated it like a baby."

"No one said anything at church?" Dave asked.

She shook her head. "Maybe they'll spill their secret soon. Meanwhile, you all feel free to eat as much as you want. I'm going upstairs to start in my old room."

"I'll help." Josh stuffed the last bite of the cupcake in his mouth and reached for his work gloves. He took the drop cloth and stepladder from the downstairs bedroom and carefully carried them up the stairs and down the hall.

"That greeny-white is for all the upper walls and ceilings," she said. "I want spring in every room."

Joshua opened a can of paint and arranged the rollers, then set up the ladder, clearly intending to paint the ceiling first. "Can't blame you. It's going to look great. A new beginning."

"That's exactly what I thought." She smiled at him, leaning on the other side of the ladder, grateful for his understanding. "Speaking of, I just remembered it's New Year's Eve."

When *Englisch* people stayed up until midnight, wished each other Happy New Year, and kissed the person nearest them.

Their eyes met. And held, as though he'd had the same thought. And something happened, silently, invisibly. Some communication in a language she'd never learned, but knew instinctively.

Joshua's voice was rough as he said, "You believe in those, don't you? New beginnings. Happy new years."

Words had vanished from her head. She nodded.

"I'm beginning to believe, too."

"You are?" she whispered. "Why?"

"Things happen around you."

"Like the clock? And the chairs? That wasn't me."

He took a step closer, one hand on his side of the ladder. "No. You. You make up your mind you're going to live here, and everyone pitches in and makes it happen. You come to be our nanny, and my mother gets pregnant."

"That happened long before I came, and your dad probably had more to do with it."

He grinned, and there was that dimple, and her hand floated up all by itself to touch it with a forefinger. His skin was so warm. With just the slightest roughness of what would be a five o'clock shadow by nightfall.

"What?"

"You have a dimple. It's distracting."

Another grin, filled with that male knowledge that probably made Eve fall head over heels for Adam. "It is, huh? Do I have another one?"

Slowly, she reached up to place the tip of her finger in the one on the other side. And then she was touching his face with four fingertips, tracing the lines of it with her gaze, and his lips parted—

—and the Yoder boys came thundering up the stairs like a pair of Clydesdales let loose in the house.

Sara jumped back, and Joshua was bending to pour paint into the tray before she could take another breath.

When the Yoders passed the door to start work in her brothers' old room across the hall, she had already begun taping off the chair rail, and the moment vanished as though it had never been.

But it had been.

She wasn't sure she wanted to put a name to it, but it had definitely been *something*. The question was, would it come again?

And what would she do?

With the Yoders right there, their sporadic spurts of conversation turned to other things. The weather was always a safe subject. Who might have been keeping the clock in a box all this time. When they might have dropped it off. Whether they should paint the exterior of the house this spring when it warmed up, or wait a year.

All four upstairs bedrooms were painted, and the hallway, too, and touch-ups done in the bathroom downstairs before she began to recover from that moment by the stepladder. Funny that it had affected her this way. She had dated in Portland, even gotten almost serious about one of the volunteer firemen, but something in her heart had always been like a rock in the road, preventing a relationship from going any further. She had thought she was committed to the *Englisch* life, but if she could commit to a cell phone and a suite in someone's carriage house, but not to a relationship, just how serious had she been?

Deep down, had she always intended to return home?

And now that she was back, had made her intentions known to the bishop and the *Gmee*, why was she suddenly obsessing over Joshua Miller? The man was two years younger, for goodness sake. Though she had to admit that he'd taken responsibility for Nathan in a way that few twenty-one-year-olds would have been capable of doing. He might have gotten the children's rhyme backwards, putting the baby carriage well ahead of marriage and certainly before love, but his family had rallied around him and faced the church with a smile and no shame whatsoever. Nathan was as welcome a Miller as the new little girl coming in the spring.

Sara's heart ached to be so welcome in such a family. Not as a nanny, or a homeless person who needed a helping hand, but as a member of it.

She rolled her eyes at herself as they buttoned up that evening, leaving a window cracked open upstairs and one downstairs so the air would flow through and take the fumes away while the woodstove kept the house warm. She'd better be careful that her fascination with Joshua wasn't just a front for her need to be part of this family. On the other hand, if that were true, she ought to have fallen for Adam or Zach, who were already members of the church and who didn't have nearly the baggage that Josh carried around, weighing him down.

Maybe that was part of the fascination, though.

He struggled with the commitment to the church just as she had. They had that in common. Where they differed was that she had come back, and he hadn't left yet.

So where did that leave her, now that she'd revealed her feelings so unmistakeably?

🦋 17 🦋

"ARE you planning to go back out to the farm tomorrow?"

It was ten minutes to midnight, and Josh had come into the kitchen with Nathan as she heated a bottle, handling pot and water as quietly as she could. Her room was directly over his and Nathan's, so he figured the baby's wail had awakened her. They hadn't planned to stay at the farm much past the time the Yoders had rolled out, but trim and touch-ups took care and concentration, and before he knew it, he had been obliged to light the buggy lamps for the drive home. Luckily, *Mamm* had held supper for them, and the whole family had gone to bed much later than usual—nearly nine o'clock.

"I'd like to," she whispered. "But you don't need to, if you had other plans for New Year's Day."

"I think it's mostly New Year's Eve that people make a fuss of. And look at us. Painting and changing diapers and heating bottles."

"It could be worse." Her face softened into that smile that came so rarely. "You could be out there driving drunk and getting arrested, like some people in the neighborhood I could mention."

"No argument there." Her face was losing its angularity and becoming a lovely oval, though those cheekbones and that nose would always give it character. And there was a calmness about her now. A settled air. He almost envied it.

She glanced at the clock over the kitchen door. "There's still time to get over to Madisons'. You'll miss the big count-down, but I'm sure they'll go most of the night."

They had received a fancy invitation a couple of days ago, addressed to both him and Sara and tucked into the Circle M mailbox without a stamp. "I just saw all those people at Christ-mas. Besides, I'd only go if you went."

"Then I guess you're not going." She smiled again, into his eyes this time, and again he felt that *zing!* in the air, like a silent thunderclap.

Nathan wiggled, and she turned away to test the bottle. "It's ready."

Usually he sat in the rocker in his room, so that he could put Nathan in the crib after the air bubbles passed. But tonight he walked into the sitting room and sat on the sofa. After a moment of hesitation, she followed him. She tucked one leg under her like a nesting crane and watched Nathan's cheeks move with his usual gusto.

"That child loves his food," she said. "He fits right in."

"He comes by it honestly," Josh agreed. "If it wasn't for ranch work, I'd be a lot heavier, probably."

"Neh." She shook her head. "Not you. You have more consideration for poor Crysanthemum."

The twins had named all their cutting horses after flowers, much to his brothers' disgust. But since the boys had been allowed to name the buggy and field horses, fair was fair. Sara seemed to like calling them by their full names—even Crysan-themum, whom Josh called Sandy out of consideration for the animal's feelings.

"If I wasn't here, would you have gone to the Rocking Diamond?" she asked curiously. "I'm sure the spread is just as massive as it was at Christmas."

He shook his head, though the only light was coming from the lamp in the kitchen and they could barely barely see each other. "I doubt it. Who would have fed our little *Nachteil?*"

"Anyone who heard him yelling," she pointed out with a certain dryness.

"But it's my job. Even though I left you in the lurch the other night."

"That's okay. Naomi came to help. But I think he likes it best when you do it. He's not as comfortable when I feed him, even though he's known us both the same amount of time."

"I guess that's how it should be," he said softly, looking down at the baby, who was beginning to slow down. He switched him to the other arm.

Sara slid over to watch him, their legs probably only touching because the sofa cushions were soft.

Or was that a sign?

"Josh?"

"Hmm?"

"Did something happen a minute ago? When we were in the kitchen?"

His breath felt heavy in his chest. "Like what?"

"Like what happened at the farm, in my old room."

Nathan turned his head away, signaling that he'd had enough, and Josh set the bottle on the low table in front of the sofa where the twins put together their puzzles. Sara handed him the cloth in her hand and he put the baby on his shoulder, patting him while he waited for a good burp.

"Only if you want it to," he replied at last.

"It isn't about what I want. You know my plans. But I don't know what you want." She paused, and Nathan burped. Josh kept patting his back while a thousand ways to answer her flapped in his head like a flock of startled starlings.

"I used to know," he finally said, for want of anything that made sense.

"Is it changing?"

Nathan had slid into sleep. "He's out. I'll put him down."

She blew out the lamp in the kitchen and followed him to his and Nathan's room, where she hovered in the doorway. The light from the lamp on the shelf above the changing table etched her face and her troubled eyes in gold, and glinted in the curls that had no covering at this time of night.

Gently, he laid the baby down and pulled up the soft, flannel-backed quilt that Malena had given him Christmas morning, though they didn't really do presents now that they were grown up. It was a patchwork of stars—yellow and blue and green on a white field. Stars to help *der Herr* watch over him while he slept, she'd said, and kissed the baby softly.

Putting his son to bed had been a small distraction. But it was clear that if he acted on those sparks between himself and Sara—let the silent thunderclap be the beginning of something new—it had to come from a sincere heart. She deserved nothing less.

She wouldn't come into his room. Here, where they had cared for Nathan's needs together dozens of times and thought nothing of it. But somehow, if she came in tonight, after she had acknowledged those sparks, it would mean something. And he wasn't sure if either of them were ready for that.

"I don't know if anything has changed," he finally said on a long breath. "I don't know what I want. A trade is one thing. I could do that, and do it well. But can I stay here and be *Englisch?*" He gazed at her, watched her face go still. "I don't know."

"You still want to be *Englisch*, then?"

He leaned a shoulder on the door frame with a huff that passed for a chuckle. "I've wanted it for years. Since I left school. I don't know how to be me and be Amish."

"You're learning to be you and be a father."

"That's different."

"Is it? Will you teach Nathan to be Amish or *Englisch?*"

He was taking fatherhood a day at a time. It was the only way he could manage it. Anything else was too terrifying. "I haven't thought that far ahead."

She nodded. "I understand. I haven't thought much farther ahead than painting the farmhouse. If I ask myself what happens after reconciliation, then after I join church, then if someone wants to court me, I start to panic. Because I don't know the woman I'll be then."

He felt her words like a hook in his heart, the way a trout must feel the moment after it bites the fisherman's nymph. "If someone wants to court you?"

She tilted her head and squinted at him. "Don't sound so surprised. It could happen."

"Phil Yoder?"

"I don't know. He seems nice. Though he's a bit like Nathan with food. It's cute in a baby, but I'm not sure I could live with it in a grown man."

He made a noise in his throat that could have been agreement—or disgust at the idea of her being with anyone else.

Anyone else but him.

Ach, neh.

The thunderclap reverberated through his spirit.

It didn't feel one bit like that moment in the kitchen earlier. It was denial, pure and simple. Because nothing could happen between them. He knew that—had known it the moment she'd talked to the bishop and told him she wanted to join church. He'd just been fooling himself all this time, enjoying himself with her and not counting the cost. Not admitting his own feelings. The truth was, he couldn't be with her because he didn't plan to stay. And if he did stay, they couldn't be together unless he joined church, too.

He couldn't have Sara without giving up his life to God. That was the bottom line.

She would never settle for anything less.

He had never wanted anyone more.

Suddenly there wasn't enough air in the room.

"Guder nacht," he said on a gasp, and pushed past her. He yanked a coat off a hook by the front door—he didn't even know whose—and let himself outside.

He stood on the porch, gripping a post as though it were the only thing that could keep him upright, and stared out toward the river. The glorious view was concealed by a curtain of whirling snow. He couldn't even see past the porch rail.

Kind of like his future.

He stayed outside, breathing deeply until the knot in his gut eased enough to let him move again. And then he walked around to the back of the house. The lamp still burned in his bedroom. Sara's was dark.

If there had been a light still on up there, he didn't know what he would have done. Walked to town again, maybe. Or gone up there and kissed those soft lips the way he wanted to.

As it was, he let himself inside as quietly as he could and hung up the coat. *Dat*'s coat, a size too big.

Josh glanced at the kitchen clock, feeling as though an eternity must have passed, but it was only twelve thirty.

Happy new year.

❧

LATER THAT MORNING, WHEN SARA WENT DOWNSTAIRS, Joshua's door stood open and his bed was neatly made. He must have slept in it, because Sara had heard him come back in, but he was gone. With a sigh, she picked up Nathan. "Would you like a bath?" she crooned. "Did *Dat* forget you get a bath before breakfast?"

She washed and diapered him and then carried him out into the kitchen.

Malena held out her arms, and kissed him all over his little face. "He's smiling!"

Sara and Naomi exchanged a glance filled with humor. Rebecca set the hot casserole on the table, and everyone sat down.

"No Josh?" Naomi asked.

"He went out to the barn," Zach said. "Said to start without him."

After their silent grace, Rebecca held out a hand for Sara's plate and scooped out a healthy helping of sausage and egg casserole. "Are you going out to the farm today, Sara?"

"I think so. If the paint is dry, I can close up the house and take the drop cloths back to the Yoders. Want to come?"

Both the twins wanted to see her progress, so Naomi said that she would look after Nathan until Joshua turned up again. Sara privately wondered if maybe he'd taken up permanent residence in the barn. All she had to do was say that little word *courting*, and he'd bolted like a cow spotting a lasso.

She and the twins hitched up Hester once the sun had come up over the rim of the mountains. Their late start had given the county snowplow time to get out, but the snow didn't seem to have stuck. It was refreshing to drive with the twins, who were fountains of information about everyone in the valley. Sara thought she was being very skillful about bringing the conversation around to the Yoder boys. After all, hadn't they both mentioned them a little too often around the dinner table?

But they turned the tables on her, and suddenly it was all about their brother Zach and Dave Yoder going to talk to the shift captain at the fire department, and wouldn't it be fun if Sara shared a shift with them and got to know Dave even better? Maybe even saved somebody's life together?

"When did this happen?" she asked, trying to slow down the flood of happy possibilities when the ones she was dealing with were quite enough, thank you. "Why didn't Zach say anything? How do you know about it?"

"We know everything going on among the *Youngie*, even Zach's little secrets," Malena told her smugly. "While you were all working yesterday morning, Susan Bontrager stopped by to visit, and told us she'd seen them there on Monday."

"Good for them," Sara managed. Thank goodness they'd arrived at the farm. "Well, I hope the department takes them on. Look, there's still smoke coming out of the chimney. That's a good sign."

When they let themselves in the front door, they found the house still warm despite the two open windows, so while Sara ran upstairs to close the window in her bedroom, Rebecca stirred up the coals in the woodstove and added a few pieces to get it going properly again. "I know we're not staying long," she explained, "but since we're here, why not be warm?" She grinned at Sara. "We can always run over to the Yoders' if we need more firewood."

"That would be taking advantage," Sara informed her. "I'll find a way to get my own wood, thank you, when I need to do more work in here."

"It looks beautiful," Malena said. "I love this yellow in the kitchen. I mean it, Sara. Once you have a sofa, I am definitely making that gray and yellow quilt for you. Do you like flying geese?"

"I like them better swimming." She wrinkled her nose at Malena, who rolled her eyes. "Whatever you make will be beautiful. I want to learn to quilt properly when you get the top done. I never had a chance to ... before."

"That's a date," Malena said.

Sara knew there was no point in checking the back porch, but she opened the door anyway. And stared. "Um, Malena?"

"What?" Malena peeked over her shoulder.

"I think that's a definite yes on the flying geese."

"What on earth ...?" Rebecca came to the door.

A wing chair sat there, upholstered in a pattern of ducks. It looked like it had come from someone's hunting cabin. Next to it was a pine dresser she recognized at once as being from her parents' room, and sitting on the dresser was a big black utility tub with a snap-on lid that clanked when Sara gave one end a shake.

"Is this what happened yesterday?"

She'd told them all about the magic arrival of the four chairs and the clock. "Yes. What is going on? Is someone playing pranks on me?"

"If it's a prank, it's a really nice one," Rebecca said. "Come on, let's get these things inside. It's cold out here."

They manhandled the chair inside and set it in the sitting room, where it looked so lonely in all that space that they took all the drawers out of the dresser to make it lighter, and lugged it in to sit against the wall behind the chair. While the twins put the drawers back in, Sara brought the tub inside and set it on the table. She popped open the lid cautiously to see a sight as familiar as her own hands.

"My mother's pots and pans." Large and small, with copper bottoms that, like the clock, had been polished to a chestnut shine. "And the bakeware." Muffin tins, cake tins, the bundt cake pan. "I don't understand."

"It has to be Rose," Malena said, hands on her hips. "Did she pack up some of your things by mistake when she and her family moved out?"

"But why not just tell me?"

"You have to admit, this is more fun," Rebecca said. "You never know what you're going to find whenever you come over."

"At least it won't be beds," Sara said. "The ones left here were only fit for the landfill, and that's exactly where they went."

"Beds are personal. You have to choose you own," Malena said. "But I don't think you'll be sleeping here for a while yet."

"Probably not until spring," she agreed. "I'll have to move out sometime to give baby Deborah a room. Unless one of you gets married and beats me to it."

Rebecca blushed and Malena hooted at the very idea. Sara put the pots and pans where they had always been, in the big deep drawers *Dat* had made to slide out. Same with the bakeware. The cookie sheets in the very bottom of the tub slid into their old rack in the cupboard over the oven. She was just considering where she ought to store the tub when they heard the sound of rubber tires crunching to a stop in the yard.

Whoever it was drove a gray Jeep that looked like it meant business. "Whose is that?" Sara asked.

"John Cooper's," Rebecca said. "The saddle maker. *Dat* took us to see him once when Buttons was two and it was time to break him to a saddle."

John Cooper crossed the yard, dressed today in jeans and a heavy coat. He might resemble Reuben Miller a little when he was older—he had that rangy, ropy look that ranchers seemed to acquire around here. Sara invited him in, and he removed his Stetson politely as he stepped inside.

"Mr. Cooper, you remember the Miller twins, Malena and Rebecca?" Sara said shyly. "They came with me today to see our progress cleaning up the place."

He shook hands all around. Sara liked him even more close up, and in a non-Madison-party setting. He had the kind of smile and brown eyes that immediately made you forget he was famous all over the country for his craftsmanship in working leather.

He took in the kitchen with an appreciative glance, and the few bits of furniture. "I like the yellow," he said. "Makes it feel warm. Good for the spirits."

"That's what I thought," she said with a smile. "We were just talking about the furniture migrating here all by itself. Some mysterious person is dropping things off on the back porch for me to find."

"Maybe folks have extra, and want to share," he suggested.

She shook her head. "That's the funny part. It seems to be my parents' things. My mother's pots and pans were here when we arrived today. Yesterday these chairs and my mother's engagement clock came back. Isn't that strange?"

His gaze met hers. "Strange ... and wonderful, don't you think? Folks are looking out for you."

"I guess they are." Almost as if she was wanted in the valley, and people were hoping she would stay. "Well, shall we walk out to the barn so you can have a look at my dad's tools? At least those stayed put, and haven't been rambling around the valley."

"After you."

She pulled on her wool coat and led the way across the yard to the barn. "The men had a work day on Tuesday," she explained as she pushed the rolling door open. "They cleaned the barn out and fixed it up. A crew went up the hill and got the water system working again." Out of nowhere, tears welled in her eyes. "They've been so kind."

"We have good people here in the Siksika," he said, following her over to the tool closet. "And I know the Amish are particularly close to each other. I'm thankful for my neighbors, the Eichers, especially when the weather gets ornery and the unexpected happens."

She opened the lids of the two rolling toolboxes and stood aside so he could examine them. He opened every drawer, taking out a tool here and there as though they were unfamiliar to him, and putting them back carefully. Finally he closed them up and stepped aside as Sara closed the closet behind him.

"That's a terrific outfit," he said at last. "What about the larger things? I'd expect to see a bench-mounted punch, or a strap cutter. A stitching bench. Things like that."

"Probably stolen," she said. "Along with our baler and some of the haying equipment. The only reason the tools are still here is because no one realized there was a closet behind that wall."

He nodded thoughtfully. "Well, if a man were buying what's in those boxes today, he'd expect to spend three thousand dollars at least. Some of those tools were likely handmade by your father, or acquired in an estate sale, because they simply don't make them anymore."

Sara hadn't expected nearly so much. Maybe she ought to roll those boxes into the house, where they'd be safer. "Thank you," she said at last. "It's good to know what you're dealing with, right?"

"I wish there was a harness maker in the valley," he said, hands on hips, as he craned his neck to see up into the rafters. "The Amish folks sometimes bring their harness to me for repair, but it's not really what I do."

Sara could see an opportunity when it was opened right in front of her, even if it wasn't really her business. "Joshua Miller is toying with the idea," she said. "He'd probably use those tools, but he doesn't have anyone to train him."

Cooper left off his study of the rafters and focused on her. "Yeah?"

"I don't suppose there's a chance you'd need an apprentice?" Oh, Joshua was going to be so angry when he heard she'd been horning in on his business.

"I already have two," he said slowly, eyeing her as though he felt the same.

The heat of a blush prickled into her cheeks. "I'm sorry. It's none of my business. I told Josh that there had to be books in the library or videos on the Internet, and he could learn that way."

"I thought the Amish folks didn't have the Internet, except maybe some of the kids with their phones."

"That's right. Josh hasn't joined church yet, so he has one. Well, I suppose he could go to Lancaster County and apprentice, but now that he has his baby son to look after, that might not be so easy."

"Joshua is a father?" Cooper's eyebrows went up. "Since when?"

"Since the middle of December. The baby's mother handed him over, lock, stock, and birth certificate."

"Wow." Cooper wedged his hat more tightly on his head. "That's an adjustment."

"The thing is, he's adjusting better than anyone gives him credit for. He actually has a knack with babies. And he's learning to love the little guy. We all are. I'm his nanny and I can't help myself."

"So he's got a good reason to want to stick around and take up a trade," Cooper mused. "Interesting." He turned with an *after you* motion, and rolled the barn door closed behind them.

When they reached his Jeep, he leaned a hip on the driver's door and gazed at her. "Would you mind giving Joshua a message for me?"

"Not a bit," she said.

Closer to the house, Hester raised her head as though wondering if it was time to go home yet. It was definitely getting colder.

"Could you ask him to come by early next week? Both my apprentices have gone home for the holidays, and I could use a hand. If it works out and he seems to have as much of a knack for the work as he does with babies, maybe I could take him on part time. I'm sure his father still needs him around the ranch, so I wouldn't want to disturb that."

Joy bubbled up in Sara's heart, and she couldn't keep the

huge smile from blossoming on her face. "I sure will, Mr. Cooper. Thank you so much."

The hat brim dipped. "Don't thank me. He'll be working his fingers to the bone." He raised his head and twinkled at her. "But if he can take up a trade here, it'll be worth it."

"I know it will. I'll tell him tonight."

"Happy new year to you, Sara." He swung himself into the Jeep.

"Happy new year. And thank you again." She lifted a hand in farewell as he swung the vehicle around and accelerated up the bumpy, potholed lane as if it were as smooth as the county highway.

Then she went into the house to try not to spill Joshua's business to his sisters until she had the opportunity to tell him first herself.

18

MALENA AND REBECCA were barely in the kitchen door when they spotted Joshua in the rocker with Nathan, and both began talking at once. Sara came in behind them and it almost looked as though she was trying to get their attention, but to no avail.

Joshua knew from long experience that trying to stop the twins when they had something on their minds was like trying to stop an avalanche from coming down a mountain.

"John Cooper came to the farm when we were there, Joshua—"

"—and he was so nice—and he likes the color you all painted the kitchen and he said—"

"It doesn't matter what he said, Malena. He was there to tell Sara what her father's tools were worth."

"And oh my goodness, Sara says it's a lot!"

"Why don't you let Sara tell her news, girls?" Naomi asked mildly from the stove. "I never heard such a pair of whiskey jacks for chatter. No one can get a word in. Take off your coats, for goodness sake, and help me get dinner ready."

But that only subdued them for about two seconds.

"Tell him, Sara, what John Cooper said."

Sara laughed as she took off her away bonnet but not her coat. "If Josh wasn't looking after Nathan, I'd ask him to help me put Hester up. I couldn't find either Adam or Zach."

Why hadn't the girls put up the horse? Josh wondered. Were they in that big a hurry to bring him their news? Joshua rose in one smooth motion and put Nathan firmly in Malena's arms. "He needs a good burp. I'll help Sara and maybe she can get a word in sideways."

He grabbed his coat and knit cap and in a moment they were both outside, where it was at least ten degrees colder than when he'd gone in an hour ago. "Thanks for the rescue. Those two are a force of nature."

"They're just excited," Sara told him. "I've got so much news that I didn't even share with them. I wanted to tell you first. I'm fit to burst with it all."

He hurried her into the barn, intrigued in spite of himself, and lit the Coleman lamp so they could see what they were doing. But when she went to unhitch Hester, who was standing patiently inside the door nibbling on the hay that had escaped a stall, Joshua stopped her with a hand on her sleeve. "Come on. Before you burst. Tell me the news."

Almost as though he couldn't control it, his hand slid up her sleeve to her shoulder, and all the bubbling excitement seemed to evaporate as she went still. "Joshua?"

"Aren't you going to tell me?" he asked, and smiled at her, and her lips parted. "After all the trouble I just went to, getting you out here alone?"

"What?" Beside Sara, the horse shifted, her hooves making a hollow sound on the floor. "You wanted to be alone with me?" Her face glowed in the lamplight, her eyes searching his.

"To hear the news," he whispered. "In a minute."

They were nearly nose to nose. Did he dare? Oh, he was a fool, but he couldn't stop. Nothing short of an avalanche hitting the barn and carrying it away would make him stop.

He tilted his head and did what he'd been thinking about for the last twenty-four hours. He kissed her.

She made a sound in her throat and leaned into him, and his arms went around her as though it was the most inevitable thing in the world. The thing he had been waiting for since he'd looked up and seen her standing next to the bar in Mountain Home, exhausted and disheveled and thin. Something about her had compelled him to help her, though now that he knew her better, he reckoned that she had really helped him.

Her mouth was soft, and so sweet, and it killed him to break the kiss, because Hester needed to be cared for. After that, they had all the time in the world.

"What about that news?" he whispered, both to tease her and to bring himself back down to earth.

"John Cooper wants you to go over to his place early next week," she said, sounding a little dazed. "To talk. Because his apprentices are away."

Well, that was coming down to earth for sure and certain. He wasn't sure whether to be amused or offended.

"Why?" he asked, his arms still looped loosely around her back.

"He thinks maybe you could work there part time. While they're gone."

He stiffened. "Wait. What? How did that happen?"

As though she realized the moment had really broken now, she stepped out of his arms. "We were in the barn. He looked at the tools and figures they're worth about three thousand dollars."

He blinked. "So much?"

"*Ja.* And then—" She fiddled with one of Hester's buckles. "And then I asked him if he had room for another apprentice."

Oh, no, she hadn't. "Sara, that was mine to do, if I was going to ask."

"I know, and I'm sorry. But he was there, and he brought it up himself about how a harness maker is needed here in the valley, and I took a chance."

He felt it again, that suffocating feeling, like something was closing in on his chest. As though he were a piece of leather, and the two halves of a vise had him in their grip. He took a deep breath, to try to fend it off.

"You took a chance. On my business."

"Well, we'd been talking about it, and he was so nice, and Joshua, he warmed up to the idea right away."

"That's great, but what if it's not what I want?"

She stared at him, perplexed. "We were just talking about your staying and learning to be a harness-maker. Last night. Don't you remember?"

"I remember it was an *option*."

Now she was really confused, her eyebrows pinched together in the middle.

He'd been stupid to kiss her. What he should have done was let her go to the other side of the buggy. Kept his hands off her. Because now he'd led her to believe— She thought— Sure as cows ate grass she'd want to make things permanent and then—

Neh. His mind wouldn't even go there. The vise was squeezing him so hard his heart hurt. He had to undo this. Go back to the way things were. Stick to his plan.

"You had no right, Sara. No right to poke your nose in my

business. You're as bad as my father, always hinting about what I should do, never paying any attention to what I want to do."

"But I thought you did want—"

"Then you should have told John Cooper I'd talk to him. Not set up a job interview. You're the nanny, not my wife!"

The color drained out of her face. "I never once said anything about—that. Never even thought it."

"Oh yeah? Then how come you're so interested in my being a harness maker? Using your dad's tools? Staying around?"

"For you, you big galoot! Not for me. What else are you going to do with yourself? You let the good-time boys down the road drag you wherever they want, and do your chores whenever it occurs to you, and hide all the rest of the time."

Now it was his turn to stare. So this was what she really thought of him!

"The only things you seem to be good at are working with tack and caring for your son." Her voice was rising now. "Don't blame me if I thought that meant you actually wanted to have a life."

"I have a life!" he shouted. "Don't blame me if I just don't want to share it with you!"

Panting, they glared at each other. Behind her, he could see Hester stepping nervously, her eyes rolling as her uneasy gaze flicked between them. He needed to end this. The time for fooling himself—for dreaming foolish dreams he didn't have a right to—was over. He had come to the end.

Turning his back on her, he stormed into the tack room and snatched up the saddlebag that held his money, a set of *Englisch* clothes, a pair of running shoes, and the guidebook to Seattle. He threw them on to the buggy's seat, took Hester by the leading rein, and turned her around.

"What are you doing?" Sara asked, the first note of fear in her voice.

He left them both standing, crossed the yard at a run, and took the steps up to the house two at a time.

"Joshua, where's Sara?" Malena asked as he loped through the kitchen.

He ignored her and practically dove into his room, where he swept up the baby bag. Fortunately Sara always kept it stocked. Her orderly habits sometimes drove him crazy, but this time—the last time—he was grateful. He stuffed Nathan's snowsuit in, too, and as many diapers as he could fit. There was a bottle of formula in the fridge, so he took it.

Now his mother and sisters were staring at him like so many owls. He scooped Nathan out of Malena's arms.

"What are you doing?"

"Going to Mountain Home," he said easily. That part was true. "It's time the Lindholms had a look at their grandson."

"But I thought they didn't—" his mother began.

He had to get out of here before his father and brothers came in from feeding the cattle. It was going to be cold tonight, so they'd be in early. The sun was already down behind the largest peak. He didn't have much time.

"Good-bye," he said, breezing out the door.

In the barn, Sara hadn't moved from where he'd left her. A look of stark horror crossed her face as he laid Nathan on the buggy seat and swiftly tucked him into his snowsuit.

"Joshua, you're not leaving."

"Don't tell me what to do."

"I mean, you're not, are you?" She moved at last, to stand in his path to the open barn door.

"Get out of the way."

"But Joshua, the baby—"

"He's coming with me."

He climbed into the buggy and held Nathan with one arm, the reins in the other hand. "Walk on, Hester."

The horse didn't move. One eye rolled back toward him as if to say, *We just got home and now you want me to go out again?*

"Walk on." He clucked to her and finally she lurched forward.

"Joshua! Where are you going?"

"I said, out of the way, Sara."

"*Neh!* I won't!" She blocked the door, both arms outstretched.

In the distance, he heard a whistle. *Dat*, calling in his brothers.

Out of time.

"Yah, Hester! Git!"

The horse surged forward and Sara leaped out of the way, gasping his name. But her frightened calls faded behind him as the buggy clattered down the lane.

Another whistle. *Dat*, probably, trying to get the attention of whoever was driving the buggy without its lamps lit. He'd light them once he was out of sight of the ranch. He couldn't take the time right now.

Nathan wriggled and protested at no longer being in the comfortable, warm kitchen surrounded by familiar faces and sounds. He let out a wail.

"I'm sorry," Joshua murmured fruitlessly. "I'll put your hat on in a minute. We have to get out of here. Now. It's over. I'm done."

But Nathan was having none of it. The volume increased, and he struggled in Joshua's grip. It was all he could do to keep Hester going in a straight line down the county highway and keep hold of his son's body. Since when had he become so strong, this little scrap?

And why had he never bought a car seat? The basket was useless now, so he hadn't bothered with it, but even that would be better than this predicament. He had not one thing for Nathan to rest or sleep in but his own arms.

Swiftly, he unbuttoned his coat, cuddled the baby against his chest, and fastened it up again. With one arm under his little behind, at least he wouldn't drop him, but now Nathan was screaming against his chest, the sound vibrating right against Joshua's pounding heart.

Get away. Get away. From her. From us. From church.

His heart drubbed in time to Hester's hoofbeats. His son screamed. It was freezing cold.

Joshua had never been so miserable nor so determined in all his life.

❧

SARA SHOVED THE BARN DOOR SHUT WITH ALL HER strength and ran out into the yard, but Joshua and the buggy were already out of sight around the first bend in the lane. She heard a whistle and ran to the fence, waving frantically.

"Reuben!" she shouted. "Reuben, *kumm hier!*"

Joshua's father rode up on his buckskin gelding, looking over his shoulder in the direction of the highway. "Who is that in the buggy?"

"It's Joshua! He's taking off with Nathan. We have to stop him!"

Reuben's attention snapped toward her. "He's what? Where is he going?"

"He's not coming back. Please, ride after him."

"Sara, you're not making sense. What do you mean—"

"Reuben!" Naomi called from the front door. She wore no coat, and both hands lay protectively on her belly. "Joshua is going to Mountain Home."

"At this time of day?" he said incredulously.

"No, he's not!" Sara shouted. "He's leaving for good. He's going to Seattle with Nathan and we have to stop him."

"Seattle?" Reuben urged the horse closer.

"*Neh, Liewi*, he's just going to Lindholms'," Naomi said. "Come in the house."

Lindholms! Is that what he'd told his parents? If he wanted to throw them off the scent, that would do it, all right. "He's lying," she said desperately to Reuben. "He might be going to Mountain Home, but it's to catch the bus."

"He would never lie to his mother's face," Reuben said grimly. "Of all his sins, that is not one of them."

"I'm telling you—"

"*Neh*, Sara, I know it's ridiculous and stupid of him, but if he feels he must see the Lindholms now, this moment, then it is too late to stop him. At least it will be warm there, for the *Boppli*'s sake. Though I'll have words for him about taking Hester out again so soon."

He reined the horse away from the fence and urged him into motion toward the barn, where Zach and Adam had already opened the gates.

Sara knew in that moment that Josh had well and truly deceived his whole family, and if anyone was going to save him from the most monumental mistake of his illustrious career in messing up, it was going to have to be her.

She ran across the yard and back up the steps to the kitchen, where she wrenched open the cupboard door and seized the cell phone in the jar. The Madison number was clearly labeled in the contacts list, thanks be.

"Rocking Diamond, this is Taylor Madison." That throaty voice was unmistakeable.

"Hi, Mrs Madison," she said breathlessly, "this is Sara Fischer, over on the Circle M. We met at your Christmas party?"

"I remember." The voice cooled. She must have got the message that the trail riding outfit wouldn't be moving to a new home.

At the dining room table, the twins frowned at each other, as though the whole world had gone mad and they were the only sane ones.

Maybe they were right.

"Is Chance there? I need to speak with him. It's urgent."

"Can I say what about?"

Oh, she was good. Nosy, but good. "It's about Joshua. I need some help and Chance is the most knowledgeable person."

"I think he's in the pool. It may be a minute before he gets here."

"That's fine. I'll wait." *No hurry. It's only a matter of life and ... life.*

By the time Chance came on the line, Sara was at the point of tearing out her barely-grown-out hair. "Hey, Sara."

"Chance, thank goodness. I need your help."

Maybe he heard the urgency in her voice. The fear. "Sure. Name it."

"I need you to drive me to the bus station in Mountain Home."

"When?"

"Now. I'll meet you at the end of the lane, okay?"

"Something wrong?"

"I'll tell you in the truck."

"See you in five."

Dizzy with relief, Sara disconnected and replaced the phone in the jar. "I'm bringing him back," she told Naomi. She shrugged on her coat, snatched the nearest hat off the coat tree—a Stetson that clearly had been left behind by someone *Englisch*—and jammed it down over her *Duchly*. She flung a scarf around her neck, and was out the door in seconds, the sound of Reuben and the boys coming up the back steps pounding in her ears like her own heartbeat.

Fleet as a deer, she ran down the lane. Just as she reached the gate with its crossbar and the Circle M brand carved by Reuben in the center, a pair of powerful lights crested the hill.

With a throaty roar, Chance Madison gunned the big truck down the highway and swerved to a stop in the mouth of the lane.

The damp highway was starting to ice up. They had to find Joshua and get the baby warm.

Sara scrambled up on the truck's high running board and threw herself into the warmth of the cab.

"Thanks," she said with a gasp, out of breath from running. "Floor it."

She got the seatbelt snapped across her body just before he did.

19

STRANGE that the waiting room of the bus station had no people in it, nor lights on, either.

Joshua drew Hester to a halt in one of the two long parking spaces against the curb reserved for the buses. He climbed out, Nathan still fretting and whimpering against his chest even though Joshua had put his little hat on, and walked up to the door, where a sign had been taped on the inside.

CLOSED DECEMBER 31 AND JANUARY 1
REDUCED HOLIDAY SCHEDULE
UNTIL JANUARY 6

Reduced to what? When was the next bus? He'd memorized the regular schedule, but it had never occurred to him to memorize the holiday schedule too. Because he had thought he'd be able to choose his moment. Not lose his head and run.

Despair showered through Joshua's insides. Not only was there no bus, and no ticket seller, he had no idea what he was going to do now. And there was poor Hester waiting in the bus's parking spot, looking as miserable as a horse could possibly look.

Nathan chose that moment to fill his diaper. The scent wafted straight up out of his coat and into Joshua's face.

He lifted his head to breathe, and saw the sky, where the gold along the tops of the snowy peaks was fading rapidly into deep blue. Stars were just beginning to prick out. No snow tonight. It would be too cold.

Now what was he going to do?

He turned and went back to Hester, leaning his forehead on her neck, both hands cradling the unhappy baby under his coat.

"I'm sorry, girl. This is no way to treat you, is it? I am so stupid that cows look like geniuses."

The horse snorted as though she couldn't agree more.

This was the end result of all his dreams. Standing in a deserted bus station with two creatures depending on him. What had he been thinking to bring the horse and buggy here? Would he have climbed on the bus and just left Hester standing, to freeze to death unless some compassionate Amish person happened by?

That's all your plans are good for. They just end in cold and death and abandonment, don't they? Because you don't think. You get an idea in your head and you can't let go of it, even when it turns out to be the stupidest idea ever.

What was the matter with him?

What had he been thinking, to run away from home? From Sara?

From the perfect life that God seemed to have orchestrated just for him?

A tear welled up in one eye and trickled down his cold cheek. For the first time, Joshua took a hard look at everything that had happened since his birthday a lifetime ago.

Der Herr had pushed Sara right into Joshua's way just when he needed her help. He'd preserved the Fischer hay farm so that she would have a way to make a living. Preserved her father's tools so that Joshua would have a way to make his. And then He'd seen to it that something magical had sparked between them, bringing it all together with such timing and skill that the significance of each piece of His plan had until this moment completely escaped Joshua.

Because he hadn't been willing to see it.

Because he hadn't been *willing*.

Oh, there was the crux of it. He hadn't been willing. Had believed his own way was so smart, so well planned, so necessary. *Well, look where that's gotten you*, he thought bitterly. *You walked away from a perfect plan in favor of ... what?*

The most crushing despair and loneliness he'd ever felt.

Nathan gave a heartbroken wail, as though he'd given up on everyone, too. Given up on Joshua, who had dragged him out of his home for no reason. In Nathan's little world, there was only discomfort and bad smells and cold, to say nothing of danger. The baby seemed to weigh a hundred pounds in Joshua's tired arms. His shoulders drooped, and despite his best efforts, more hot tears escaped, trickling down against Hester's warm neck.

Come unto me, all ye that labour and are heavy laden, and I will give you rest. The words of Jesus came into his mind like the softest whisper. *For my yoke is easy, and my burden is light.*

But the Amish yoke wasn't easy. It was heavy. It was more than a man could bear. There was so much that required obedience—*Uffgeva*—and Joshua had never been good at that.

It's better than this, his heart whispered. *Think of all that God has done for you. The happiness that is waiting for you. All you have to do is say yes to Him.*

"Help me," he whispered brokenly against Hester's neck. "Help me."

Cast all your care upon me, for I care for you.

He couldn't do this alone. Suddenly he saw it with the kind of clarity that came on winter mornings when you could see forever. If he chose to leave, he'd be alone. No family, no God, no love. He'd have Nathan, but what kind of a life would he be carrying him into? This poor baby had already been abandoned once. Was Joshua going to compound that by going to some strange place and handing him over to strangers to look after?

What kind of man would do that to someone so helpless?

I care for you.

Joshua cared for Nathan. Loved him. *Ach, mein Herr, what have I done, taking him away from You? From love?*

From Sara?

And there was that thunderclap in his heart again. For the first time, he recognized it for what it was.

Love. I love her.

He straightened, pulling Nathan more tightly against his chest. "I love you," he told the baby, and kissed his wet face. Wet with tears that Joshua had caused. "Forgive me. It's going to be different now. I love you, and I love Sara, and for once in my life, I know what to do."

SARA DIDN'T HAVE A WORD TO WASTE ON CHANCE MADISON. Her entire being strained forward ahead of the truck, ahead of the headlight beams, scouring the road for the glimmer that would be the reflectors on the back of the buggy.

"Sure he's gone to the bus station?" Chance finally asked as they passed the last mile marker before Mountain Home. Scattered lights told her they were approaching the northern edge of town. "Not to the Lindholms'?"

"He took all his money with him," she said tersely. "What does that say to you?"

"It says he needs to check the schedule," Chance said easily, one hand draped over the top of the wheel. "Buses don't run on holidays."

That got her attention. "They don't?" Hadn't she arrived on a Sunday? But no, that wasn't a holiday.

"Nope. I wish you'd told me on the phone where he was going. If he just turns around and goes home, you'll have dragged me out of the pool for nothing."

"He might go to his friend's."

"Who, Ty Carson? He went skiing this weekend."

What would Joshua do if all his means of escape were taken away? Would he realize that the hand of God was doing exactly what it had done for her? Closed off all the roads until there was only one way left.

The way of obedience. Of embracing what they were both meant to be.

The way that meant a life of joy and love and family and useful work to do.

"There's still the car, though, if Ty didn't take it." Chance sounded thoughtful, but Sara came back to herself with the feeling that he was needling her. Playing on her worry.

"We'll check both places. Slow down, would you? The speed limit is thirty-five in town."

"Telling me what to do, missy? After I'm doing you this big old favor?"

"Yes."

"I don't take kindly to that. Why can't you be a little nicer?"

"Why can't you be a man instead of a kindergartener?" she snapped. "Look out, that's a stop sign."

Deliberately, he stomped on the gas pedal. And three things happened at once.

She was thrown back against the seat.

The lamps on the side of an Amish buggy glowed as it started through the intersection.

And all she could see in the glare of the headlights was the buggy flying—the horses dragged off their feet—a blanket wrapped around a baby as it cartwheeled through the air—

❦

JOSHUA HEARD A WOMAN SCREAM AS A BIG FORD TRUCK roared through the intersection like some prehistoric animal pursuing its prey. It missed the back of his buggy by a good five feet, but still, Hester leaped forward and it was all he could do to get her under control and guide her down the street and into the safety of Tyler Carson's front yard.

He had to get Nathan inside. Inside, and cleaned up, and warm, and then they'd go back to the Circle M where they belonged.

Except the house was dark and the Swinger was gone.

So was Mrs Carson's Toyota, which meant she was probably at some New Year's Day party.

His heart sank. "I'm sorry, *mei sohn*," he said on a sigh, "but it looks like you're going to have to be stinky for a couple more miles."

Wouldn't you know it—the minute he made up his mind, suddenly everything conspired against him, as though the

Deiwel himself had got wind of it. He wouldn't blame Hester one bit if she refused to take another step. Her head hung down, and it was clear she was close to done.

Then she lifted her nose and her ears turned in the direction of the street. He heard it himself—the throaty growl of a big truck. Maybe the same one that had nearly hit them. Or maybe it was a hunter, and he was lost.

What had happened to the woman who had screamed?

The growl came down the street and the truck—good grief, it was Chance Madison's big Ford—jerked to a halt at the curb, sliding a little on the slick asphalt. The passenger door was flung open and a woman in a Stetson tumbled out of it, screaming something at Chance that Joshua's stunned brain couldn't piece together.

He climbed out of the buggy just as Chance stomped on the gas and fishtailed off down the street.

"Joshua!" the woman cried, and ran into the yard.

Sara.

"Oh, thank the *gut Gott!* You're alive!"

She flung herself against him before Joshua could stop her, and Nathan let out a screech and another cloud of baby diaper scent. Sara jumped back and clapped her hands to her nose.

"He needs a change," Joshua managed to get out before she keeled over, hands on her knees, her shoulders shaking, and the most terrible sounds coming from her throat. "Sara—Sara, I wouldn't have gone. I'd have come home, I promise you. Sara, can you hear me? It's all right. I'm coming home."

She lifted her face to his—a face streaked with tears and a terror in her eyes that he could only pray he would never see again.

"I thought he hit the buggy—I thought you were dead—the baby—I thought—"

"Stop, *Liewi*," he crooned, and stinky baby or not, he pulled her against him so that Nathan was warm between them. "He missed by five feet. If that was Chance, he never would have hit the buggy. He's too good a driver for that."

"He's lost all the hearing in his right ear, I'll tell you," she choked out. "From me screaming."

"Serve him right," Joshua said. *"Bischt du okay? Sara?"*

"Ja," she said, her chest heaving. *"Ja,* I'm okay. I thought I would die of fright—but I'm okay. It was a flashback. What I saw. Oh, Josh, I thought I was done with those—I never want to go through that again."

"You won't. And if you do, I'll be right there with you to help you." She snuffled into the shoulder of his coat. "We need to get the two of you home, but I don't think Hester has five miles left in her today, thanks to my stupidity."

"Do you know someone closer?" she said, lifting her tear-stained face. "Someone who won't mind two half-crazed people landing on them?"

"I do," he said, his voice soothing. Comforting. "Rose Stolzfus, who owns the quilt shop—she lives three houses along. Her son Alden has his blacksmith shop in the barn, and I bet Hester will appreciate someplace warm and dry after all her efforts."

Her breathing began to even out. "I met Rose at church. I liked her. You keep Nathan where he is, and I'll walk Hester. I hope she can make it."

Together, the three of them and the horse made it the last quarter mile, only to find Alden already out in the yard, his own buggy horse half harnessed.

"Joshua—Sara!" he said in astonishment. "I was just coming to look for you."

"For us?" Josh repeated, unable to take it in. His brain must be seizing up.

Alden laughed and took Hester's leading rein. "Reuben called. All the *Gmee* in Mountain Home are on alert. Here, I'll take Hester and Hephaestus back into the barn. You two go into the house. Once *Mamm* lays eyes on you, she'll let everyone know you're safe."

Safe. Joshua would never forget again how great a gift that was.

Sara's hand found his and, still holding the baby under his coat, they walked to the little house and up the steps. Rose Stolzfus threw open the door, and warmth and light spilled into the Montana night in glad welcome.

20

"ARE you certain you want to go through with this?"

Once again, it was after midnight and Sara and Joshua were looking after Nathan, not because Joshua couldn't do it on his own, but because Sara hadn't been able to sleep. Tomorrow was church Sunday, and reconciliation.

He nodded, settling into the corner of the sitting-room sofa to feed Nathan while Sara dried the pot in which she had warmed the formula and set out the sterilized bottles for tomorrow, when they'd mix up a new batch.

"I want to do this with you," he said as she came to join him. "I've sinned, too, and if I'm going to start baptism classes with you and my sisters, I want the road cleared of all its rocks beforehand."

"I guess if you've already told Little Joe, and he agrees, then it's going to happen," Sara said at last. She settled beside him with one leg tucked under her, leaning against his side while the woodstove in the kitchen warmed all three of them with its glow. "I have to confess I'm glad. Going through it alone would be hard."

"We'll face the hard things together from now on," he said softly. He didn't have a hand free, but the look in his eyes was as good as a caress.

"It's what this family does, isn't it?" she whispered. "Faces things together, sacrifices together, celebrates together."

"I hope you're not saying you think of me as a brother," he joked.

Sara raised her gaze to show him how very far from the truth that was, and from the intensity that deepened in his, it was clear he understood.

"I want you to be part of this family," he said in a rush, as though he'd been holding the words in.

"I already feel like I am." Sara smiled down at Nathan, who was halfway through his bottle already.

"I mean for true," Joshua said. "I mean as my wife."

A fountain of joy seemed to burst inside her, illuminating the room, the ranch, her very future. She could hardly breathe with the wonder of it. He'd told her, of course, about his revelation that freezing night at the bus station. About the perfection of the heavenly plan that had been put into motion for them. She had no doubt whatsoever that marrying this man was God's will for her. And she wanted to more than anything.

"Sara?" A note of anxiety crept into his voice. "You want that, too, don't you?"

She cuddled into his side and reached up to kiss that beautiful angle at the intersection of his jawline and his ear. "I was looking into the future for a second," she said. "And I was struck speechless. Because I'm so happy."

"Is that a yes, then?"

He looked so adorable, half hopeful, half confused.

"It will be a yes," she told him slowly, thinking it through.

"Once we've been reconciled and baptized, it will be a yes. But not until then. Don't you think that's best?"

After a moment, he nodded. "All things in their time." Then he grinned. "How am I going to wait for spring?"

"The same way I will. With you. Here. Together." And she felt perfectly free to stretch up again and kiss that dimple right where it lived.

They sat contentedly together until Nathan finished his bottle. Joshua shifted so that the baby lay on the towel draped over his shoulder, and patted his back gently.

"While we're talking about the future," he said, "have you thought any more about the *Dokterfraa*'s letter?"

Naomi had written to Reuben's relatives in Whinburg Township asking for Sarah Byler's address, but Carrie Miller had done more than that—she had taken the request over to her home in Willow Creek, and Sarah had written back herself.

Dear Sara,

I hear by way of Carrie Miller in Whinburg that you are an EMT, and you're also interested in learning the ways of herbs and the craft of the healer. I'm not certain about what kinds of herbs grow out there in Montana, but my son Simon tells me that the growing season in the high country is very short—in some places only three months. And I thought Pennsylvania had long winters!

So you are living at the Circle M ranch? As you know, Daniel Miller is staying with Carrie while Lovina Lapp sells her antique business to her sister-in-law. The house is sold, much to her relief, and I believe they are just waiting to give the keys to the new owners before they begin their journey west and their new life together with you all. Simon is engaged to Cora Swarey from the Amity church district in Colorado. They expect to marry next winter, after he has had a solid year of training as a blacksmith. Then he hopes to open his own shop in Amity. Do you know the Swarey family and the Colorado churches?

Weddings are such happy things. Sometimes I wonder if Simon and Cora think I will be an interfering mother-in-law, and that's why they're settling so far away! But Simon assures me that's not so. He loves the high country, he says, as much as Cora does. He went out there to work a couple of summers ago and it changed him. He says it's because the altitude took him closer to God, and maybe that is so. My sister-in-law Amanda Yoder married Joshua King from Amity—do you know his parents Savilla and Wilmer? It seems their family are all boys, and Joshua is the first to marry.

Anyway, I'm sorry to chatter so much! There is romance in the air and I've only been married to my Henry a short time, so I'm still susceptible to the charm of it.

I will be sending along a package with Daniel and Lovina to help get you started in learning about cures. The herbs I'll send are the very basics that I count on, so you will want to replenish them. I'm also including a copy of my recipe book, and encourage you to begin your own, even as I was encouraged by Ruth Lehman, the Dokter-fraa to this district before me. You see how we form a kind of chain, passing our knowledge to the daughters of our spirit—the spirit of care for God's people. I will also incude a list of books I have found helpful, and copies of letters from other healers I have been writing to in the brief time I have been doing this. Ruth Lehman, I must say, is very well connected and she has shared her correspondents with me. Now I am sharing them with you.

I hope we will have a lively correspondence, and that someday when we are visiting out west we might even have a chance to meet.

Your sister in Christ,
Sarah Yoder Byler

Sara had practically memorized the letter since it had come at the beginning of the week. Sarah Byler was definitely going to have a regular correspondent.

"I have been thinking about it," Sara said softly now to Joshua. "Every time I do, I get a warm feeling inside, as though Sarah has invited me to Sisters' Day or something close to it—people all working on the same thing for the good of someone else."

"EMTs do that, too," Joshua said. Nathan had fallen asleep after his labors, but Joshua made no move to get up and put him in his crib.

They were far too comfortable here on the sofa, the three of them, in the midnight hour.

"I know, but ..." Sara paused.

"But?"

"Maybe if Dave Yoder and Zach join the volunteer fire department, there won't be such a need for my help," she said. "I can still help them study for their licenses, though."

He straightened a little to gaze into her eyes. "You wouldn't be an EMT? But I thought that was what you wanted to do."

"I've been thinking about it a lot. I want to keep my license, because the bishop said I could, and why let it lapse when it could be useful? But if I can learn to be a *Dokterfraa*, and run the hay farm, and we have Nathan and the harness shop ... oh, life will be so *gut* and so busy I don't see how I'll be able to be an EMT too."

"You're sure? It's your decision."

"I'm leaning that way."

He nodded, and she felt a spurt of relief that he had left it up to her. Just as she had learned that when it came to things like harness-making and apprenticing with John Cooper, she had to leave it up to him.

"Do you like being a part-time apprentice to John?" she asked. "Even now that his regular apprentices are back?"

"I do like it," he said. "I want to learn everything I can, as quickly as I can, so that I can support the three of us in the future."

"The three of us," she said, laying her head on his shoulder. "I like the sound of that."

"So do I," he whispered. "Only the *gut Gott* knows how much."

❧

THE PREACHER CONCLUDED HIS SERMON AND INSTEAD OF announcing the closing hymn, Little Joe Wengerd got to his feet.

Rebecca Miller felt the breath back up in her chest. The moment had arrived—a moment the entire *Gmee* had known would come today.

"Today, before we sing, there is a matter to be dealt with," the bishop said. "Today a young man and a young woman have requested that they be reconciled to the congregation. I have agreed to their request even though they are not yet baptized and therefore it is neither necessary nor even customary. Baptism, as we know, washes away all the past and leaves us clean and new in the sight of God. These young people could have said nothing and simply allowed the water poured out on them to wash away their sins."

The bishop paused, and Rebecca felt as though he was looking at her as his gaze passed over his flock.

"But it has been revealed to me that forgiveness goes both ways. And that we as the body of Christ must ask ourselves if we have been as much help to these *Youngie* in their need as we could have been." He made a beckoning gesture with one hand, and Joshua rose from his place with the unmarried young men. Sara, who was sitting next to Rebecca, joined him to walk up the center and kneel on the plank floor in Will and Dinah Eicher's sitting room.

Dinah sat on the end of the bench closest to where Sara had sunk to her knees. Smothering a sob, she reached over and clutched Sara's shoulder. Her head bowed, Sara covered her friend's hand with her own.

They stayed that way even while the bishop said, "Sara Fischer, repeat after me."

Sara said softly, repeating the bishop's words, "I come before this congregation in the sight of God to ask forgiveness for the willfulness that did not cause but did contribute to the deaths of my father, my mother, my two brothers, and my sister. I pray you will forgive me, for because of my actions, a home containing the Spirit was lost to the church."

The bishop lifted his head and along with the members of the *Gmee,* said, "We forgive you. Forgive us."

"I forgive you," Sara whispered. She laid her cheek briefly on Dinah's hand, and when she raised her head and met the young woman's gaze, cleansing tears rolled down both their faces.

The bishop turned to Joshua and instructed him gently to repeat his words.

Rebecca had expected Josh to mumble. But while his head remained bowed in humility, his voice was clear and unmistakeable.

"I come before this congregation in the sight of God to ask forgiveness for the sin of fornication, which is expressly forbidden by Scripture. I pray you will forgive me, and help me in the spirit of Christ to raise my son Nathan to obey God and love his people."

"We forgive you. And we will," Rebecca murmured along with the rest of the congregation, and heard Malena's quiet voice beside her.

They had failed Joshua somehow, going about their own busy lives and hardly even seeing how unhappy he was. If it hadn't been for Nathan and Sara, she and Malena would have lost their youngest brother forever to the world. In her heart, Rebecca vowed to be a better sister. To look around her and really see when someone was in need. To give when it was necessary and let the light of God's love in her life shine through her like a lamp.

"Please rise and return to your seats," the bishop told the kneeling pair.

Rebecca slid over and made room for Sara between herself and Malena. And as Little Joe announced the final hymn—a hymn of joy and reconciliation—Rebecca felt Sara straighten her back and sing as though a burden had fallen from her shoulders. As though she had only joy to look forward to now that the way was clear.

Rebecca's throat closed and cut short a long note. Sara and Joshua had found love in the strangest circumstances. If the whole family hadn't been convinced beyond a doubt that God's hand was in it, Rebecca wouldn't have believed it even yet, when it was right in front of her. But there was no doubt that her wayward brother and this broken, outcast young woman were made for each other. Both healing now. Both no longer outcast, but looking forward to restoring that once empty home to the church.

Ja, the old house on the hay farm was empty no longer. Over the past week, furniture and household goods had continued to migrate back to it as though they had legs of their own. Rebecca had heard whispers that when Rose Stolzfus had moved out, members of the church had quietly put the Fischers' things in storage in their own homes, waiting for the time they would be needed again. Sara had given up trying to catch people in the act of returning things in order to thank them. She just accepted the slowly filling rooms and cupboards with a grateful heart.

Thinking of it, Rebecca's own heart ached with longing to have what her brothers had—Daniel, with the woman God had brought back to him after he'd let her get away. Joshua, with the woman God had guided to him that cold winter Sunday when she'd stepped down off the bus. When would it be Rebecca's turn? Would she even accept another man's love if it stood in front of her? Or was she just going to keep pining fruitlessly for the man she'd seen across a room when she'd visited her cousins in Colorado last summer?

She didn't even know his name, because she hadn't had the courage to ask. She'd just gazed at him while the heavens parted and the angels sang ... and he'd gone home after singing as blind to her existence as she'd become alive to his. She still dreamed about him at night—romantic, impossible dreams that somehow involved a kiss that she'd never experienced in real life.

Was it love when you missed someone you'd never met? Maybe she should ask Sara.

But she knew she wouldn't. Rebecca was the quiet one of the Miller siblings. The one no one noticed. The one who made everyone comfortable and then seemed to disappear.

She wasn't the kind who attracted notice, especially from young men.

But oh, just once—just him—wouldn't it be wonderful?

THE END

AFTERWORD

NOTE FROM ADINA

I hope you've enjoyed my second book about the Miller family. If you subscribe to my newsletter, you'll hear about new releases in the series, my research in Montana, and snippets about quilting and writing and chickens—my favorite subjects! Visit adinasenft.com to sign up, and be sure to browse my other Amish novels set in beautiful Whinburg Township, Pennsylvania, beginning with *The Wounded Heart*.

To find out what happens when Rebecca's dream comes true, read the third book in the Montana Millers series, *The Amish Cowboy's Bride*. Here's a sneak peek.

The Amish Cowboy's Bride

How can you dream about a man you've never met?

Rebecca Miller is the shy twin, the thoughtful twin ... the invisible twin next to her vibrant sister Malena. She's content to dream of a man she saw but never spoke to the previous summer—until one stormy winter night when she rescues an unconscious accident victim and recognizes him instantly as the same man.

Noah King and his family arrive in Mountain Home to find his brother Andrew in a coma and a young Amish woman by his bed, holding his hand. They know he's in love with someone, but his *Rumpringe* has been so wild they never dreamed it would be an Amish girl. With huge relief, they welcome her instantly as a future member of the family. At least, his parents do. Noah can't help but feel that this quiet girl is far too good for his handsome, restless brother. As she spends time with his family, she comes to embody everything Noah dreams of in a woman ... but now can never have.

The Miller family on the Circle M did not see this coming. Rebecca engaged to one of the King boys from Colorado? How did this happen? And when Andrew finally wakes up and has no memory of her, the only person who knows it's not amnesia is Rebecca. With Andrew believing they're engaged, too, she could have everything she ever wanted simply by saying nothing. But the more she comes to know Noah, the more she realizes she might have been weaving her dreams around the wrong man ...

Look for *The Amish Cowboy's Bride* at your favorite online retailer! —*Adina*

GLOSSARY

Spelling and definitions from Eugene S. Stine, *Pennsylvania German Dictionary* (Birdboro, PA: Pennsylvania German Society, 1996).

Words used:
Aendi: auntie
batzich: crazy
bidde: please
Bischt du okay? Are you okay?
Boppli, Bopplin: baby, babies
Bob: bun; hairstyle worn by Amish girls and women
Bruder: brother
Daadi: Grandfather
demut: humble
denki, denkes: thank you, thanks
Dochder, Dochdere: daughter, daughters
Dokterfraa: female herbal healer
Duchly: headscarf
mei Fraa: my wife

der Herr: the Lord

der Himmlischer Vater: the heavenly Father

Englisch: non Amish people, also their language

Gefunnenes: foundling

Gmee: The church, the local Amish congregation

Gott: God

guder mariye: good morning

guder owed: good afternoon

guder nacht: good night

gut: good

ja: yes

Ja, ich komme: Yes, I'm coming

Kapp: prayer covering worn by plain women

Kinner: children

Kumm hier: Come here

Kumme mit: Come with me

Liewi: dear, darling

Loblied: The traditional second hymn sung in the Amish service

Maedel: maiden, young girl

Maud: maid, household helper

Mamm: Mom, Mother

Mammi: Grandmother

Mei Gott, hilfe mich! My God, help me!

mei Hatz: my heart

mei Sohn: my son

Nachteil: night owl, screech owl

neh: no

nix: short for *nichts*, meaning, *is it not* or *ain't so?*

Ordnung: discipline, or standard of behavior and dress unique to each community

Rumspringe: "running around"—the season of freedom for

Amish youth between sixteen and the time they marry or join church

    Schweschder: sister

    Uffgeva: giving up of one's will, submission

    verhuddelt: confused, mixed-up

    Was ischt? What is it?

    Wie geht's? How goes it?

    Youngie: Amish young people 16 years and older

The Smoke River series

Grounds to Believe

Pocketful of Pearls

The Sound of Your Voice

Over Her Head

❧

The Glory Prep series (faith-based young adult)

Glory Prep

The Fruit of My Lipstick

Be Strong and Curvaceous

Who Made You a Princess?

Tidings of Great Boys

The Chic Shall Inherit the Earth

❧

Writing as Charlotte Henry

The Rogues of St. Just series (Regency romance)

The Rogue to Ruin

The Rogue Not Taken

One for the Rogue

A Rogue by Any Other Name

ABOUT THE AUTHOR

USA Today bestselling author Adina Senft grew up in a plain house church, where she was often asked by outsiders if she was Amish (the answer was no). She holds a PhD in Creative Writing from Lancaster University in the UK. Adina was the winner of RWA's RITA Award for Best Inspirational Novel in 2005, a finalist for that award in 2006, and was a Christy Award finalist in 2009. She appeared in the 2016 documentary film *Love Between the Covers*, is a popular speaker and convention panelist, and has been a guest on many podcasts, including Worldshapers and Realm of Books.

She writes steampunk adventure as Shelley Adina; and as Charlotte Henry, writes classic Regency romance. When she's not writing, Adina is usually quilting, sewing historical costumes, or enjoying the garden with her flock of rescued chickens.

Adina loves to talk with readers about books, quilting, and chickens!
www.adinasenft.com
adinasenft@comcast.net

Made in United States
North Haven, CT
05 April 2024

50939332R00145